Someone was watching

A chill, as raw as the pain in her throat, tore through her. She turned to the trees. Someone was watching. No crack of a branch under foot, no cough, no rustle could warn her. It was a sixth sense. Intuition, and vision sharp as a cat's kept her poised, frozen over her handlebars. She stared at the woods until the greens and grays of leaves, branches, and shadows swam in front of her. The foliage seemed deeper, darker, impossibly thick without her friends. She shouldn't have let them go.

HEAR NO EVIL

Death in the Afternoon
Missing!
A Time of Fear

HEAR NO EVIL

Death in the Afternoon

Kate Chester

SCHOLASTIC INC.
New York Toronto London Auckland Sydney

ISBN 0-590-67326-2

Copyright © 1996 by Leslie Davis Guccione.
All rights reserved. Published by Scholastic Inc.

12 11 10 9 8 7 6 5 4 3 2 1   6 7 8 9/9 0 1/0

Printed in the U.S.A.   01

First Scholastic printing, July 1996

To the Reader:

Sara Howell is profoundly, postlingually deaf (meaning she lost her hearing after she learned to speak). She is fluent in American Sign Language (ASL), and English. She can read lips.

When a character speaks, quotation marks are used: "Watch out for that bus!" When a character signs, *italics* are used to indicate ASL: *Watch out for that bus!* Quotation marks and *italics* indicate the character is signing and speaking simultaneously: *"Watch out for that bus!"*

Unless the sign is described (for example: Sara circled her heart. *I'm sorry . . .*), the italicized words are translations of ASL into English, not literal descriptions of the grammatical structure of American Sign Language.

HEAR NO EVIL

Death in the Afternoon

Chapter 1

Sara Howell shivered under the canvas canopy. The heavy August mist settled on the flower arrangements that framed the casket. The liquid air draped the cemetery and hovered over the river. Even the repaired and re-opened Shadow Point Bridge was nearly invisible. Sara looked away.

She'd left the church in a downpour, but by the time the limousines had wound their way through the gates of Riverside Cemetery, the rain had dissipated to a drizzle. The metal seat of her folding chair pressed the back of her legs. She was cold, the kind of cold that hugged her bones, despite the season.

To her left, her four grandparents talked

among themselves. To her right, her brother Steve brushed the crease in his pants, then stood to talk with Father Bingham. Sara shivered again as they glanced at her. When he'd finished with Steve, the rector patted her arm and smiled. Did he really think she could smile back?

Beads of moisture slid along the satin-lined hood of his brocade cope. The ceremonial cloak was reserved for special occasions, he'd told her confirmation class years earlier, for celebrations, sometimes a very important funeral.

Sara pushed her long brown hair from her face. Grief burned and her pulse raced. She wanted to run, to bolt through the crowd until she was free of all the well-intentioned, curious mourners who'd come to bury Lt. Paul Howell.

After words with her grandparents, Father Bingham adjusted the velvet clasp at his neck and walked across the grass to his place at the head of the burial plot. The breeze fought its way off the Buckeye River and lifted the edge of his cloak until Sara could see the muddy toes of his shoes. The wind rippled through the flowers and scattered petals that had filled the heavy air with the scent of gardenias and roses. Her grandmothers held their hats. She rubbed one bare leg against the other to fight her gooseflesh.

A line of parked cars snaked out of sight down toward the bridge, and out to the cemetery entrance. Mourners still arrived under taut, black umbrellas. They bobbed and hugged, leaned to her grandparents, whispered to her brother as they had at the church. So sorry. Such a senseless accident. Strangers. Sara searched until she found Keesha Fletcher and Liz Martinson, the only two who were there exclusively for her. If only they could be on either side of her under the canopy.

Behind Keesha's family a phalanx of police officers formed stiff, dark rows as far back as the trees. The mist gave their hats a pearly luster. Hundreds of officers and officials had come from as close as the Penn Street precinct and as far as the state capital. It had taken three weeks to make the arrangements for the service. All this for Lt. Paul Howell, and he hadn't even been killed in the line of duty.

The attention comforted her grandparents. Sara closed her eyes and took deep breaths. She was due back at Edgewood. After a summer at camp, she'd been packing for the return to her boarding school. It was halfway across the country, a cocoon her father had thought would keep her removed, safe. Removed from reality, maybe, but safe from grief?

She ached for the limousine that had brought her here from the church, a sliver of privacy in the most public day of her life. She should be behind dark glass, behind the windshield wipers that had fanned left and right against the downpour. Clear, blurry, clear, blurry. From the church to the cemetery, her view of Radley's city streets had matched the rhythm of the blades. Behind her ribs the ache burned. It moved into her throat and the back of her eyes. Don't cry; don't cry.

She made a half turn but her brother put his arm over her shoulder. The protective gesture surprised her, but when she looked up at Steve, his expression was stoic, as usual. In the three endless weeks that she'd been home, he'd been hardly more than a shadow. She understood. They were separated by six years, her residential school, and very different lives.

Steve was in charge. The furrow between his eyebrows, the tight set of his mouth masked his handsome features. He had stopped dating. He didn't sleep. He looked older than twenty-two and was always tired. Steve dealt with their grandparents; Steve talked to the press; Steve made the funeral arrangements. He'd cleaned out their father's desk and returned the last of his files to the Radley chief of detectives. Sara wanted to help, had tried to make her grandparents understand that she would stay in Radley.

There'd been furtive glances and closed-door conversations. They said Steve was in no position to take over . . . hardly out of adolescence himself. A bachelor with his own social life . . . a detective with crazy hours. Edgewood School was more home to her than Radley; a refuge; every need was met; life was smooth. Clear, blurry, clear, blurry. Her future was like the view through the windshield.

Even now under the canopy there were only distant cousins and grandparents. They were all too young, too old, or too far away to replace what she'd lost. Sara faced the truth: nothing would *ever* replace what she'd lost.

Half a mile west on the lane that meandered down under the bridge to the Shadow Point Marina, an anonymous coward had destroyed every scrap of stability in her life. She was glad the view was lost in the haze. Ashes to ashes; dust to dust. That's all she had left inside. She stared at the flowers. Clear, blurry, clear, blurry.

Grim-faced police officers were everywhere, enough to keep the press away. Instead it heightened their frenzy. Radley Senior Detective Lt. Paul Howell had been killed by an unidentified hit-and-run driver. Cowardice. Death. Intrigue. It was like blood to sharks. Reporters hung out in her apartment lobby at Thurston Court until the Fletchers shooed them away. Now they jumped hedges at the cemetery.

The entourage was set up on the other side of the privet hedge that separated the burial plots from the open lawn. Father Bingham was ignoring them, but Sara watched. Somebody aimed a telephoto lens down the bluff toward the boats. The scene of the accident from the site of the burial. How artistic. Couldn't the officers from the precinct arrest anyone with a camera?

Sara recognized an anchorwoman as the one Steve had refused to talk with at the hospital. She'd practically arrived with the ambulance. Even at this distance Sara could read her lips as she spoke to her viewing audience. "Three weeks and Lt. Howell's killer still remains a mystery. The unsolved death leaves two orphans. Their mother" — the reporter glanced mournfully to the headstones — "died five years ago. Stephen, a rookie detective on the Radley force, is left to fill his father's shoes. Sara is still a teenager and will now finish her adolescence without the guiding force of her father who was instrumental in helping his daughter overcome her . . ."

Sara turned her head and cringed at the melodrama. Anger flared. It was almost pleasant to feel something besides the anguish that clawed at her ribs. She wasn't about to "finish her adolescence" as some pitiful orphan. What she'd overcome was no business of any reporter. She'd never let anyone pity her and she wouldn't start now. As for Steve filling their father's shoes, that newscaster and anyone else might as well know she had every intention of majoring in criminal justice at the best university she could get into.

Steve motioned for her to stand and turn around. The mourners watched the hill behind her. Some were crying. As scheduled, on the rise behind the plot, a bagpiper stood alone on a jagged rock. His mouth puckered on the blowpipe. She watched his fingers move along the chanter. The wind lifted the pleats of his kilt and the tassels on his kneesocks. Mist swirled.

The piper blurred despite Sara's blinks and she wiped her cheeks. Steve raised his arm as if he might tuck her back into the crook of his shoulder, but stopped. Don't be brave for me, she wanted to tell him as he stayed stiff.

When the piper finished, the mourners turned back to Father Bingham as he raised his hand; hundreds of heads lowered. Steve's jaw tightened. Her grandparents fought for composure. Sara was numb, as if she'd been trapped in this suffocating mist since the first awful night when they'd met the ambulance at the hospital.

Father Bingham signaled her. It was time. She took roses from her chair and tried to step forward with Steve, but as she turned to him, his shoulders sagged. He slumped and buried his face in his hands.

Alarm propelled her. She put her arm around his back, afraid he would shake off her grasp, but instead he put his arm across her shoulder and straightened up. They took deep breaths together. She handed him a rose and when he was back at attention, they stepped forward and finally placed the flowers on their father's casket.

Even back under the canopy, her brother's eyes stayed riveted on the roses. He looked straight ahead and spoke. She didn't understand. She shrugged and raised her eyebrows. As Father Bingham offered the closing prayer, Steve looked at her. Tears stained his face, but he brought his fingers to his lips then dropped his hand to his open palm. *Thank you.*

It was over. Mourners pressed forward around her grandparents. Police officers surrounded her brother. She searched for Keesha or Liz but umbrellas were as thick as the mist. The cemetery swirled with humanity. Loneliness tugged at her until her heart thundered. She tried to think about the limousine, cool and dark and safe, but her pulse pounded. She was as flushed as she'd been cold, then lightheaded. She moved toward her brother, barely visible through the crush of officers, but by the time she caught his eye, her knees buckled. She put her hand out. Steve caught her as she crumbled.

Sara filled her lungs with the leathery scent of the limousine and opened her eyes to her brother's concerned expression. The color came back into his pale complexion and he said something to the driver. The car slowed.

Her numbness began to fade. Maybe she wasn't alone. Maybe together they could make sense of the senseless. In one fluid motion, Sara signed. *No more Edgewood. School here. Life here. Family.* She tapped her chest, opened and closed the fingers of both hands, signed *Y* and dropped her hand. *I want to stay.* She brought her fists together in front of her and pointed to Steve. *With you. My family.*

Chapter 2

Follow me. Sara straddled her mountain bike long enough to sign to Keesha Fletcher and Liz Martinson. She pressed her hand against her pounding heart, then grabbed the handlebars and pushed off, through the stone gates that marked the entrance to Riverside Cemetery.

In the weeks since the funeral, Sara had waited for the internal message that would send her clearheaded signals that she was ready, that it was time. There was no signal, just a feeling that coming back to the cemetery might dull the sharp edges of her grief. She hadn't told Steve where she was going.

Since her grandparents had agreed to let her stay in Radley, her remote, distracted brother had transformed himself into surrogate father, watchdog, tutor, and guardian. His good intentions clung to her like the funeral mist. Despite his concern, this was something she wanted — needed — to do without him.

Instead she'd asked Keesha. They'd been best friends since the Fletchers had moved across the hall of Thurston Court when they were both five. Sara and Keesha went to kindergarten together and that spring when Sara got meningitis and lost her hearing, Keesha had begged to study American Sign Language with her. They created each other's name signs. *K* plus linked fingers, the sign for *friend,* meant *Keesha. S* plus *friend* meant *Sara.*

When they were fourteen, Keesha had introduced her to Liz and together they chose *L,* plus a crooked index finger pulled down from her mouth for *red,* for her name sign, a salute to her coppery hair and favorite color.

Sara pumped the bike pedals and took a curve at a racing angle, letting the wind whip up under her helmet. A flock of starlings rose up off the lawn and scattered overhead. She tried to remember their raucous sound, but during her six years of hearing, she'd never paid attention to birds. Shrill? Sweet?

From deep in her childhood she could call up the pleasure of her mother's lullabies, but in the ten years she'd been deaf, her father's "voice" had evolved into the typed-out messages on her TTY, the telecommunication machine that augmented the telephone, and most recently the computer and her E-mail.

During her years at the Edgewood School for the Deaf, especially since the death of her mother, she'd "read" her father's voice in their daily chats. He'd been her link to Radley. Despite the difficulties of giving up the school and plunging into the hearing world, she couldn't go back.

Sara slowed at the intersecting lanes in front of the plot that had so recently been a mass of flowers and mourners. It was still raw from the broken earth. No crowds, no well-meaning friends and respectful police officers, no snooping reporters. She looked over the empty lawn as it sloped away to the woods that separated it from Shadow Point

Park. She found the spot where the piper had stood. Deep shade and dappled sunlight replaced the mist. A cardinal landed on the headstone. Already carved in honor of her mother, it now told the world that both of her parents were here. She waited for emotion to rise up and swallow her, but there was nothing but thumping in her chest and steady, simmering anger that somewhere on the crowded Radley streets the careless driver was still free.

Sara felt the gaze of her friends as they waited. Keesha's eyes were as brown as her skin, Liz's pale blue; both stares were sympathetic. Her friends spoke to each other. Sara fought the urge to tell them to stop. At Edgewood she was never excluded, never the outsider. All that had changed. Everything had changed.

Sara grabbed her bike and threw her leg over the bar. Liz said something, but she was at an angle and Sara couldn't read her lips. Liz should turn, full face. Liz should know better by now! Sara pushed off, scattering birds, face to the wind.

The girls caught up and rode single file as

Sara left the lane for a trail opening into the woods. The air was instantly cooler, calming. The bike jostled over the pine-needled ground and occasional root. There was a shortcut here, somewhere, that led back to the sidewalks and city bustle outside the cemetery gates, but Sara was in no hurry to find it. Instinctively she followed a jogging path that forked and disappeared under the trees. Bright patches of blue overhead peeked through the branches until the trail sloped into Shadow Point Park. The ride was cool, pleasant, distracting. She pedaled the length of the trail and glided into the sunlight.

DANGER WARNING DANGER
TRAIL TO SHADOW POINT CLOSED
DO NOT TRAVEL BEYOND THIS
LOCATION

The moment she saw the sign and the barriers she knew exactly where she was. They were in a clearing on the edge of the riverside park, at the first footings of a bridge that ran from Radley across the river to Hillsboro.

Well over their heads the steel and iron girders of the Shadow Point Bridge crisscrossed in graceful arches that spanned the parking lot, the marina, and the Buckeye River.

It was too late to turn around or to avoid the remnants of construction debris, the only reminder that Shadow Point Bridge had been repaired. Sara tugged off her helmet, shook out her hair, then hit her forehead with the heel of her hand. Stupid, she said to herself as her friends followed into the September sunshine. Keesha leaned her bike against a tree and looked out over the Buckeye River, but Liz wheeled up next to Sara.

Sara circled her heart. *Sorry.*

Because she was deaf, Steve said she could read movement in eyebrows and lips as if they were instruction manuals, but even a hearing person would have known that Liz was upset.

On the other side of the barriers damaged crossbeams and junked tie rods awaited removal. Repair construction tarps still hung in some of the girders to keep debris from plunging into the river below. The way the cars had, Sara thought with a grimace.

The northeast section of Shadow Point Bridge had collapsed a year earlier on a hot August day when Sara was home between camp and her return to Edgewood. She and Keesha had been in the Martinson pool when Liz's mother screamed while watching the noon news. A section of the bridge had collapsed; three cars plunged into the river. Rescue efforts were only partially successful and five people had died. Keesha explained the significance to Sara when Liz got out of the water. Martinson Engineering Company had built the bridge.

Even back at her boarding school, Sara had hounded her father for updated information. When the accident reports and investigations kicked in, she was relieved when her father sent her E-mail to say that there were no signs of negligence; no criminal charges would be filed against Mr. Martinson. That didn't ease the fact that when Sara came home for Thanksgiving, the bridge still gaped like the hungry, open mouth of some steel and iron monster.

At the bend in the Buckeye, the old fashioned riverboat *Buckeye Queen* steamed into view, the boat the Martinsons had reserved for an upcoming party. Hastily Sara tried to divert Liz's attention. *Your parents' riverboat party is soon. I can't wait. The vibrations on the deck are great for dancing. Better than the school gym.*

"I didn't understand any of that," Liz muttered.

Sara read her lips and held her breath against her frustration. She did some quick, silly dance steps in the grass, then pointed again to the riverboat. "Great for dancing." Sara spoke this time.

In reply Liz tapped her watch. "Whatever. I didn't mind going to the cemetery, but I had no idea you would drag me practically under the stupid bridge of all places."

Again Sara slapped her forehead and circled her heart.

"Yeah, well I guess it was stupid. Think about somebody else for a change."

A flush crept up from Sara's collar. Angrily she pointed up the river to the marina. "Somebody else? Why come here on purpose? *Dad was killed right there in the park-*

ing lot. You think I'd come here on purpose!" As always she added ASL for emphasis.

Liz shrugged. "Forget it. I have a baby-sitting job in an hour. I need to get home and clean up."

Sara gave her their sign for *See you at school tomorrow.*

"Sure, if I'm even there tomorrow, or ever, for that matter."

Sara signed to Keesha. *What does she mean?*

Keesha tried to talk, but Liz started off on her bike.

Sara tapped Keesha's shoulder. *Go home with her. Make sure she understands I didn't mean to lead us this close to Shadow Point.*

"What about you?" Keesha asked.

I'm not ready. I want to ride around some more. When Keesha looked skeptical, Sara added, *School or bridge. She'll talk to you. Find out.*

Keesha looked reluctant, but she nodded. "I guess I'd still be upset, too, if it had been my dad's company that built the bridge and then it collapsed and killed five people."

Chapter 3

Sara let Liz and Keesha go. She stood with her bike and watched the *Buckeye Queen* steam slowly around the bend and out of view. Out over the river birds caught the air current and drifted. She watched one soar, up to the bridge trusses, then dive nearly to the water. Pleasure boats drifted. She moved to the edge of the trail. The marina opened in front of her. She could see the boat shed and the sun glinting off the cars parked in the lot under the footings of the bridge. People were everywhere. Just like that Black Saturday . . .

Her throat was raw and tight, and the hot sting in her eyes sprang up unexpectedly. A boat marina at dusk on a summer Saturday — Steve said their father's car had been parked next to the bridge footing. She found the spot easily. There, away from view, no witnesses to the accident, just people who had heard the screech of tires. She brushed back the tears. She should have stayed in the cemetery. What on earth had made her take the woods and a trail she hardly knew?

A chill, as raw as the pain in her throat, tore through her. She turned to the trees. Someone was watching. No crack of a branch under foot, no cough, no rustle could warn her. It was a sixth sense. Intuition, and vision sharp as a cat's kept her poised, frozen over her handlebars. She stared at the woods until the greens and grays of leaves, branches, and shadows swam in front of her. The foliage seemed deeper, darker, impossibly thick without her friends. She shouldn't have let them go.

Limbs swayed. It was the same soundless wind that had come off the water the day of the funeral. She thought of Father Bingham's cope and the bagpiper's kilt. The Buckeye River breeze had teased them the way it swirled around her and changed directions now. Although the wind rose off the water, it suddenly pushed her along the path, away from the woods, the cemetery, and the imaginary eyes she envisioned. It was as if the wind were calling: follow me.

Damn. Sara signed the expletive and scolded herself for the chills and the fear. She shook her head to clear it. This independence was what she'd wanted, what she'd convinced Steve and her grandparents she was ready for. She could just imagine what her brother and grandparents would think if they knew she was on a closed trail looking for hostile eyes in the trees and messages from the wind.

She rubbed her arms to chase the chills and started off on her bike. She wouldn't go back by way of the cemetery, but not because of some foolish premonition. She knew the parkside trail by heart and once she traversed the parking lot, it was easier to get back to Thurston Court and Radley's east side by way of the marina.

The only obstacles were the debris. Technically the trail was only closed under the bridge. When she reached the warning sign, she hoisted her bike onto her shoulder, grateful that she'd worn her gloves. The bridge was repaired; the rubble was neatly piled. Whatever danger there'd been from construction was long passed.

Sara walked carefully. The breeze died and her chills and premonitions along with it. The air grew cooler as she moved into the shadow. She rested briefly by leaning — bike and all — against the granite base of the bridge's first arched span. She looked up at the infrastructure and thought again of Liz Martinson. Hopefully Liz would open up to Keesha on the ride home and explain what had upset her.

Sara took a deep breath and hoisted the bike again. This time she winced as the bar bit into her shoulder and the pedal scraped her calf. She hurried. Twenty more feet and she'd be back in the daylight and able to ride. She took half a dozen steps and stopped. Something wasn't right. Eyes; she felt it again in her scalp, under her helmet, and across her shoulder blades.

She shivered and then broke into a sweat. Something I ate, Sara thought, and pressed her stomach. She stood long enough to catch her breath. The breeze came, up along the ridge, around the granite as if the currents were fingers. It brushed her legs and her shoulders again. Follow me. This time fear made her suck in her breath. Gooseflesh still tingled under her helmet. She looked up. Something moved. Up in the girders, the filtered light faded to grays and blacks. She saw a leg. Shoulders. Something — someone — had pulled back into the shadows.

A sudden blur caught Sara's eye. Something was falling, fast, soundlessly from the girders. Sunlight and the clear afternoon were just a dozen steps in front of her. The breeze stayed insistent. She rushed out of the shadows, gasping for breath as she put down her bike and felt the rhythmic pounding of her pulse in her ears.

Her back, shoulders to hips, tingled as if someone were about to grab her. She whirled around. Behind her the dirt swirled. A miniature tornado spun itself out as the breeze died. On the path where she'd stopped and leaned against the granite base, jagged pieces of scrap metal lay scattered, dropped from the infrastructure above. If there had been noise, a warning, she couldn't have heard it.

"Hey!" She craned her neck and called in her muffled voice. She put one hand in front of her mouth and the other over her vocal cords. She called again, sure from her breath and throat vibrations that she'd made sound. Fear settled bone-deep, but there was no response to her shout except pigeons that flapped their way into the daylight.

Sara mounted her bike and hit the trail at top speed. As she raced, she took the first hairpin turn with her leg out to balance the rakish angle of her bike. Her speed forced her to concentrate and she sped along the empty path clearheaded, focused on the path and the spectacular view from Shadow Point.

She navigated the second turn and didn't stop until she reached the edge of the river. Again she maneuvered around warning signs that the trail was closed. The bike path merged with others that snaked along the water so that when she arrived at the picnic area, no one would have known which path she'd taken.

Families filled picnic tables; children climbed on playground equipment; teenagers hung out together. Sara straddled her bike and watched the activity, avoiding the parking lot at the edge of the grass. It was laid out under the second arch of the bridge and ran from the picnic area of Shadow Point Park to the buildings at the edge of the water. A restaurant, dock for the *Buckeye Queen,* and full marina lined the river.

She looked back at the woods that served as a buffer from the cemetery. Traffic moved across the bridge. Sara shielded her eyes and watched. It began again. At first the wind teased. It started at her calves, then her shoulders, and down her arms. Follow me. She held her breath as if that might slow her hammering heart. She shook her head: No. "No." A gust threw a tendril of hair across her face.

Don't cry; don't cry. Hundreds of people; broad daylight. She got back on her bike and pedaled through the parking lot. She rode past the far corner of the lot where her father had been parked. He'd been walking to his car, here at the back. Just as Steve had said, the bridge footing obscured the view from the picnickers, yet from the top of the trail, under the bridge, she'd been able to see the spot clearly. No witnesses here.

Fists with pointed index fingers thrusting at the ground . . . the ASL gestures for *here* appeared in her head. She pedaled away, a gust flattening her shirt against her back. She scanned the lot, barely aware that she was riding in and out of cars.

Chapter 4

Radley's cityscape twinkled through the narrow kitchen window as Sara grabbed an apple from the refrigerator. Tuck, her golden retriever, trained as a hearing-ear dog, nudged her, indicating that the phone or doorbell was ringing. Sara glanced at the wall phone. The small light was blinking. It changed to a steady light, however, indicating that Steve had answered. She ruffled Tuck's neck in a thank-you.

She and Tuck had been around the block twice. She'd finished her math assignment. She'd even emptied the dishwasher and cleaned up the kitchen in an effort to ease her restlessness. Grief from visiting the grave, confusion and embarrassment over Liz's reaction at the bridge, fear she'd get caught carrying her bike through the closed trail — any number of things could have caused her attack of anxiety and nerves at Shadow Point. She chided herself as she closed the refrigerator and stared at the invitation stuck on the door with a carrot-shaped magnet.

Gloria and Patrick Martinson
invite you to celebrate the twenty-fifth
anniversary
of Martinson Engineering Company
aboard the *Buckeye Queen*
Saturday, September thirtieth
Seven P.M. until midnight
Departure from Shadow Point Marina

One of the things Sara missed most about her father was the way he got right to the heart of a problem, his detective's way of honing in on a situation. She closed her eyes and tried to blot out the mental image of his headstone, the metal signs at Shadow Point, the shadows in the repaired girders.

Sara left the kitchen distracted and deep in thought. She shivered over the possibility that something in her subconscious had led her to the bridge and the scene of her father's death. She would never have gone intentionally. She signed *school or bridge* to herself. She had enough pain in her own life without dwelling on Liz Martinson's behavior, but right about now it helped to think about somebody besides herself.

Common sense, girl! was one of Keesha's favorite signed expressions. Sara needed a dose from her best friend, but the Fletchers had gone out to dinner.

A hand on her shoulder made her jump. Steve cupped her chin, his way of telling her he wanted undivided attention as he struggled with sign and making himself understood. "What gives?" He repeated her signing: *"Upset about school or bridge?"*

She signed, *Nothing,* and hoped he wouldn't go into his I'm-your-big-brother-and-legal-guardian-which-makes-me-responsible-for-you routine. Adjusting to Steve took work, almost as much as adjusting to living in Radley and attending a hearing school. He was often hard to understand, often wrong with his gestures. In his rush to accept responsibility for her, he wanted what felt like hour-by-hour reports.

Nothing! he signed back and dropped his hands. His handsome features were expectant, his blue eyes clear. "Something. You've been pacing and restless since you got home." Steve signed again. *Beside the point. What gives? School trouble?*

No.

Dad?

No. Quickly Sara made a zero with her thumb and index finger.

"What kind of detective am I if I can't even get information out of my own sister?"

She spoke and signed to make sure he understood. *"A good one. Like Dad. Don't worry. I don't need a cop; I need common sense. Liz, Keesha, and I rode bikes to the cemetery."*

Cemetery!

"I'm okay. Not the problem. We took the Shadow Point trails afterward. Liz Martinson got very upset. Nothing to do with you."

Steve looked startled. "You were with Liz Martinson?"

She nodded. "Yes, Liz. The bridge. *Very upset with me.*"

"Bad reminder for her." He flushed. "For you, too, Sara."

She raised her hands to sign, to describe winding up there by accident, to ask what — or who — made that scrap metal fall. One look at her brother made her stop. Steve was a cop, not a psychologist, a cop already overly concerned with her every move.

He put his arm around her shoulder. "Right now you need to focus on adjusting. New life. New school." He signed *New* and shrugged. "And helping me sign."

"Liz hasn't been upset like this since the bridge collapsed."

"You shouldn't have been there, not even in the cemetery. Too soon." *Too soon.*

Not me. I worry for Liz. She was irritated that he kept changing the focus away from her friend.

Steve shrugged. "Liz has a TTY. Maybe she'll call. Talk to her about it in school tomorrow if she doesn't."

"She might not be in school tomorrow."

Steve's flush deepened. He arched his eyebrows and in reply Sara arched her shoulders: I don't know, either.

Steve circled his heart.

Sara nodded. She was sorry, too.

Steve looked apologetic. "I'm going to take a shower and change. I hate to leave you at night this soon, but that was the station on the phone. I need to go in."

Don't worry. I'll be fine, she signed too rapidly. "I better get used to it." *One more thing . . .*

He tapped his watch.

I know, you have to go. It's about Dad. The marina . . . this afternoon . . . a wind came up, same as the funeral . . . She fumbled with her hands as she fumbled in her head.

"I miss him, too, Sara, every day."

She nodded. *Somebody must know something.*

"Leave it to the police. To us." Her brother sighed and headed for the shower.

Sara nodded and wished she could ask him to stay home, not leave her by herself. It was too soon. Still restless, she snapped on the television in the room that had been her father's bedroom/home office. She closed her eyes and took a deep breath, hoping for a trace of aftershave, or even the aroma of the old rug or the new draperies he'd ordered at Christmas. Maybe too hastily she and Steve had replaced the bed and dresser.

A couch, coffee table, and comfortable chair filled the space, but it was still cluttered with reminders, from candid photos to Paul Howell's favorite books. She and Steve wanted it that way, a place where they could still feel his presence.

Tuck settled into his favorite spot at the foot of the couch and Sara scanned the TV channels with the remote, barely taking time to read the captions on the programs. As she waited for a commercial to end, she pulled a book from its place on the bottom shelf of the bookcase behind the easy chair. *Historic Parks and Gardens Along the Buckeye River.* Shadow Point Park, ablaze with tulips, narcissus and flowering trees filled the cover, under a thin layer of dust.

Tuck suddenly put his paws in her lap. Startled, she looked at the desk phone and TTY. The blinking light became steady.

Steve must have the portable phone in the bathroom. She waited for her pulse to settle. Before . . . She tried not to think about her father always being the one to answer the phone, always the one to be called away on police business.

Sara went back to the book and idly flipped the pages from back to front, familiar with many of the award-winning gardens laid out in full-color plates. Her program began and she was about to close the book when she hit a page marked with a paper clip. The page on the left was a shot of the Shadow Point Park fountains. On the right was the landscaping surrounding the bridge, pink and purple with blooming rhododendron and dogwood. She recognized the area immediately. It was the same view as she'd had that afternoon when she emerged from the woods onto the closed area at the base of the bridge.

Her program started. She needed to read the captions to follow the story line so she tossed the book back on the shelf with one eye on the TV screen. It wasn't until fifteen minutes later when the second set of commercials began that she realized a manila file had slid out from the back cover of the book.

Sara pulled the folder into her lap. As far as she knew neither her father nor Steve had much interest in gardens, certainly not enough to keep a file of clippings or related articles. The book couldn't have been her mother's. The bridge had opened after her death and since it was featured in the Shadow Point section, that meant the book was new.

She opened the folder. *Poke around some more* was written at the top of a sheet of legal paper. It was in her father's familiar handwriting, scrawled over sets of doodles and sketches. The room was still, but gooseflesh raised the hair at the nape of her neck as if that Shadow Point breeze had snaked its way in over the windowsill.

Chapter 5

The ceiling light blinked as Steve came through the doorway, one hand on the light switch. He was in jeans and sneakers and looked as though he were still a criminal justice student at Radley University, rather than a detective on assignment. Undercover, she thought, but knew better than to ask.

He gave her his familiar searching look. She'd been so engrossed in the file and the scrap of paper she'd forgotten the television.

"School night. Don't stay up late." He pointed to her lap and shrugged for an explanation.

Sara held the file out to him. The minute Steve took it, she began to sign. *Dad's! Bottom of bookshelf.* "Old file."

"Old file?" He looked at the yellow lined paper and shook his head. "You're right. Old. There's no tab — label on the outside. It's not with the others we cleaned from his desk. One scrap of paper doesn't make a file, Sara."

Sara tapped the paper that had held her attention. *Poke around some more.* "Almost like he left us a message." *A message for us, Steve.*

Color drained from Steve's complexion, then returned. This time his flush filled his cheeks. Something wasn't right.

"You know what this means?"

"No. Nothing. Probably written years ago." He shrugged. "Not even with Dad's papers."

"Not years ago! The book is new. You know something." She pointed at his still-bright complexion, pulled her index finger from her chin and ran both hands at the sides of her face. *BLUSH!*

"Forget it."

"Why? What is it that made you look so shocked?"

"Nothing."

"Something!"

Steve sighed so hard she saw his chest rise and fall. "Nothing," he said. *Nothing*. "I'm not over his death, yet. That's all."

Say again. Sara started to get out of her seat, but Steve put his hand on her shoulder. "We have to go forward, Sara. On with our lives. Dad would want that. I hate that he's gone and I hate the way he died. No leads. No trail. No witnesses. I hate it, but that's the way it is. Understand?"

Yes. She understood too clearly. He didn't want her anywhere near anything that hinted of police work. This was no time to get into an argument. She shook her head. "Okay, forget Dad. I'll pretend the note means I should find out what's bothering Liz."

Steve faced her so she could read his lips. "Don't pester where you shouldn't. Liz might want privacy. Dad's note means you should poke around your homework assignments more."

She dragged her thumb out from under her chin; pulled her index and middle finger from her eyes. *Not funny*.

Steve frowned. *Say again*.

"Serious stuff!"

Sara! His sign was edged with anger. "I'm due at the station and I can't go to work and worry about you all night. Forget this." He held the file open. "Our lives are complicated enough. Don't make something out of nothing. Look, there's no label, no papers. It's not a file. It doesn't mean anything."

She stiffened, turned her face, and ruffled Tuck's fur.

Steve cupped her chin to make her read his lips. "I mean it. Whoever hit Dad is now a criminal for not stopping or turning himself in. Leave it to the police. Don't play detective." He dropped the folder into the wastebasket. "If I put in a full shift, I won't be back till you've left for school tomorrow. Turn on your bed vibrator or the light flasher to wake up. Will you be okay alone? Can I work without worrying about you?"

Worry about the bad guys, she signed, attempting humor. *I'm independent.*

Steve brought his fingertips to his lips, then to the palm of his other hand. *Thanks.* He juggled his house keys as he left.

* * *

Her program was over; her dog was asleep; and her adrenaline was still pumping. Time dragged with nothing but her thoughts for company. She pressed her fist to her stomach. "It's a gut feeling," was one of her father's favorite expressions. When he had been the lead agent on a case, he said it was his own internal instinct that made something feel suspicious, feel wrong, even feel right. Sara fought the familiar ache in her throat and tried to ignore the gooseflesh that raised her skin across her shoulder blades. It was after ten. She should get ready for bed.

Sara got up to leave the room, but stopped at the den door. The apartment was dark, a mass of shadows down the narrow hall in both directions. Steve had turned on a single lamp around the bend in the foyer when he left, but there was no more than a pool of dim light through the darkness. The bedroom doors were shut; the shadowed living room suddenly seemed cavernous.

She sucked in a breath. So much for feeling independent. Creepy sensations and lunatic breezes at Shadow Point, falling debris, and now a scribbled note in a picture book, and a paper clip that coincidentally marked the area where she'd been that afternoon . . . There had to be other things to think about. She left Tuck asleep and scurried across the hall to the bathroom.

She yanked on the faucets and wished she'd taken her shower before Steve had left. She wished she could just tell him not to work the night shift, not to leave her, not yet. At Edgewood she'd rarely thought about her father's and brother's police work. It was as much a part of her as being deaf. Deaf. She glanced over her shoulder into the hall, then closed the bathroom door. At Edgewood everything was geared to the *deaf* community. No isolation. No fear. At Edgewood she never worried.

She was unable to pinpoint what kept her skin cold and her heart racing. It was impossible to tell if Steve's reaction to the file had been a brother's or a rookie detective's. Something had made him flush. Steve was the one who had brought up their father's death. The criminal aspect. Leave it to the police.

The hall bathroom was small, with a single

vanity and tiled shower stall. One of them could now use their father's master bath, but neither was ready to take it over. She got out of her clothes. As the water heated, she moved the portable phone Steve had left balanced on the edge of the vanity. Just like Dad; never without the phone.

She stayed under the hot spray longer than necessary, and hoped the pounding stream of water would clear her head, give her answers, calm her down. When there wasn't an inch of her left to scrub she turned off the water.

She'd stayed in so long that even with the fan running, the small room was steamy. As she dried off, she glanced at the mirror. ADAM ST. was printed in capitals in the misted glass. Small droplets of condensation drooled from the bottom of the letters, but the faint message was still clear: ADAM ST.

ADAM ST. Her brother had scrawled the message on the mirror in the middle of his shower. She wiped the glass guiltily. Steve was right. He had enough to worry about without her pestering him over an ancient scrap of paper. It didn't matter that he was out. He wouldn't have answered her questions. In sign or English his reply would have been: None of your business.

She toweled off and pulled on her nightgown, then turned the blow-dryer on her hair. When she finally opened the door, she nearly knocked Tuck over. Her retriever bounded from his spot in the hall, sending her back against the toilet, as if he'd been trying to get to her for hours. When she regained her balance, he lead her down the dark hallway toward the front door. Her heart stayed in her throat. Tuck had been trained only to alert her to strangers.

It was nearly eleven. She stopped in the hall, unaware that she'd pressed herself against the wall until she hit the back of her head. Tuck turned the corner and his shadow lengthened as he reached the lamp on the table next to the front door. His tail stopped wagging. She inched forward, to the corner. Tuck was crouched, riveted to the door. The knob turned. The light above the buzzer stayed dark as someone tried to enter without knocking. Sara watched the slowly turning doorknob.

Chapter 6

Sara yanked a ceramic dish off the foyer table and stepped back into the dark hallway. She hadn't even remembered to throw the chain in the lock after Steve left. Tuck came back to her; nudged her thigh. Yes! She knew someone was at the door.

Her hands were cold and clammy. From her angle it was impossible to see if her brother had thrown the deadbolt. The door inched open, no chain to hold it. Tuck tensed, ears flat to his head. Sara's heart skipped, then pounded painfully against her ribs. She raised the dish as a dark hand reached for the dog. Blood rushed to Sara's face as she recognized the wedding band. Familiar and friendly. Tuck's ears relaxed and Brenda Fletcher entered the foyer.

Keesha's mother looked at Sara's raised hand and circled her heart. *"I'm sorry!* Now I've scared the life out of you. I was afraid of that. We just got home and there was a phone message from Steve to check on you before you went to bed. Fiasco."

Say again.

Brenda Fletcher nodded, familiar with many of Sara's signs. "I came over and hit the buzzer. I could hear Tuck barking, but when you didn't answer, I worried and let myself in. You were in the bathroom. I heard the dryer." She pantomimed drying her hair. "I thought it would scare you to death if I opened the bathroom door, so I let myself back out, and waited ten minutes." She smiled sheepishly. "Here I am. And you're still terrified."

Sara fanned her burning cheeks. *It's okay. Thank you.* "Tuck brought me to the door. I'm fine. Really. I — didn't know anyone had a key. . . . Steve shouldn't worry."

"He's trying to be the perfect guardian."

And giving me heart failure in the process, she wanted to add, but didn't.

Mrs. Fletcher pantomimed driving. "Want a ride in the morning? Keesha's coming early with me for her piano lesson."

Sara managed a weak smile. "Too early. I'll walk." She signed *Good night* and waved her neighbor back across the hall.

As soon as the door was closed, Sara set the chain. She knelt and pressed her face into Tuck's fur and bit back tears of relief, then turned on a dozen lamps. She finally fell asleep after midnight with them all blazing.

Steve's room was still empty when Sara's bedside lamp flashed to wake her for school. She snapped off the apartment lights she'd kept on all night, not one bit grateful for her brother's misguided concern. She could have hit Keesha's mother over the head, or worse.

In the clear light of morning she tried to convince herself that Steve's advice and explanation for the "file" seemed reasonable. If she hadn't ignored the warning signs at the bridge, there would be no coincidence of the marked page in the book being the same trail she'd taken down the hillside to the marina. Besides, it was a trail hundreds of people biked when it was open and was photographed in every season.

She wolfed down breakfast, pulled on her school uniform of green plaid kilt and white polo shirt, then added her crew jacket, a windbreaker with crossed oars and *Radley Academy* emblazoned across the same green plaid. Sara had rowed for Edgewood and joining Radley Academy's crew had been Liz's idea. Wearing the jacket helped make her feel accepted, and was a tradition as it had been at Edgewood.

Little else was the same about the two private schools. Keesha's mother Brenda Fletcher was head of the Radley Academy Lower School and had convinced Sara's grandparents and Steve that with its individualized programs, Radley had a place for her. As an administrator she had even been able to arrange for financial aid. She'd also found an interpreter to accompany Sara to class and sign as the teachers spoke.

Keesha and Liz helped take the edge off oeing new, but there wasn't much they could do about her being different. Sara put Tuck on his leash, slung her backpack over her shoulder, and left for Radley Academy looking just like everybody else. She wasn't just like everybody else. She was an orphan. Her brother was a cop. She was deaf.

This was what she wanted, she reminded herself daily as she fought the isolation imposed by kids unaware that she read lips and could understand them only as long as they spoke directly to her. She loved the beauty and ease of American Sign Language, but she could speak, as well. She knew her voice was muffled and odd, but they could understand her if they tried. She could — would — fit in.

The morning traffic was thick as Sara left the lobby and handed her dog over to John O'Connor. The Thurston Court doorman had walked Tuck since he was a puppy whenever the Howells were too busy or their schedules too erratic. It reminded her that John O'Connor also had a key to their apartment.

The older man moved his left fingertips

from his lips to his palm, then brought his hand up under his right wrist: *Good morning.*

Sara gave him a thumbs-up for the effort.

She left Thurston Court and crossed the avenue alone, since Keesha had gone early for her piano lesson, with her mother and her older brother Marcus. Their apartment building and Radley Academy were in the residential part of the city Sara liked best. A quarter of a mile west on Penn Street, just down from Steve's precinct office, Buckeye Foods had their bakery. When the wind was right, east Radley smelled like chocolate, vanilla, even cinnamon and nutmeg.

Townhouses had small pockets of lawn; late-summer flowers still bloomed from window boxes and clay pots. Each city block was divided down the middle by an alley that led either to old-fashioned garages or off-street parking spaces.

This Monday morning she hardly saw — or smelled — any of it. Her late-night visitor had only been a neighbor, but it reminded her of how vulnerable she was. Life in Radley would never be the way it had been, or the way it was in Edgewood. From now on she would be on her own — alone — a lot.

Something compelled her to look over her shoulder. She shook off a chill but kept walking as she glanced down each alley, along the roofline of low-slung garages and their closed doors. She thought about her brother on a stakeout along dim lanes and warehouses in the high crime neighborhood near the docks. ADAM ST. It was impossible to shake the prickly sensation that had plagued her since the bridge, the feeling that she was being watched.

She tried to relax by studying people as she walked. Making up stories about strangers was a game she'd played with her parents and brother as a child. They'd invented stories in sign to help them all learn their new language. She'd taught the game to Keesha, too. She passed a group of commuters waiting at the bus stop and remembered her father's favorite.

Zoo keeper. His elephant is missing and he's out looking for it. Rich old lady, Steve might add. *Smile. Act polite, Sara. She's going to give us a million dollars.*

ASL sometimes became their secret language. She adjusted her backpack and spotted a middle-aged woman holding a briefcase and finger spelled to herself. *J-E-W-E-L T-H-I-E-F. Briefcase full of diamonds.* She stopped abruptly as the ache spread up through her ribs. It might have calmed her jitters, but it was too soon for a game so much a part of her father.

As the city bus approached and the woman got on, a man stepped from the alley farther up on her left. He held a cigarette between his teeth as he studied the townhouse garden closest to him, then knelt and adjusted a camera. He had on a jacket with *Radley Gazette* on the breast pocket. City photographer, she thought. But that hadn't taken any imagination.

He stayed on one knee, strap around his neck, with the telephoto lens focused on the flower bed. She passed him. He was no more than a blur in her peripheral vision, but her sixth sense was unmistakable. She felt him pivot, aim his lens directly at her as she passed, then pivot back to the flowers.

Sara's heart leaped. She gripped the straps of her backpack and forced herself to stare — and walk — straight ahead. She'd been right all along; she was being followed.

Common sense, girl! She envisioned Keesha and her flying fingers as she tried to calm herself. The press had hounded her family, put them on the evening news before her father had even been buried. No one ever asked; none of them thought about how she or Steve might feel; they just chased the story they thought the public wanted.

Deaf Orphan Makes New Life at New School. She crossed the next intersection and imagined the headlines of yet another story on the Howells, this one with pictures. Let it go, Steve would have told her. She did, unwilling to take the chance that the photographer might not understand her muffled speech.

The grid of streets stretched east to the academy campus then out to the Buckeye. She crossed at the light, but chills continued to creep over her shoulder blades. After half a block she turned around. The photographer was gone. Her head swam. Sara filled her lungs slowly. Go to school. Meet Keesha. Concentrate on what's bothering Liz and forget about yourself. She crossed the next intersection and scanned the groups of students heading for the campus. There was no sign of the familiar red hair.

By second period Sara and Keesha were in biology class. There was still no sign of Liz. Mr. Hagstrom lectured from his desk; Sara's interpreter Suzanne Andrews translated . . . *the estuaries that feed the Buckeye River, and the balance created . . .*

With less than ten minutes left, Liz Martinson entered the room and, without a glance at anyone, opened her book and stared at the chalkboard. Even from two rows away, the flush in her fair complexion was apparent. Mr. Hagstrom kept speaking. Mrs. Andrews kept signing. Sara blushed as her interpreter tapped her arm, then tapped her own forehead and raised her index finger. *Paying attention? Understand?*

Sara nodded and circled her heart.

The minute class finished, Liz bolted. Sara was a ball of nerves as she thanked Mrs. Andrews, agreed they'd meet again for English, and hurried into the hall where Keesha was waiting.

Girls' room, she signed as they watched Liz disappear through the door at the opposite end of the hall. The corridor was jammed, made worse by a class of kindergartners winding their way like ducklings through the Upper School to the library.

What gives? Keesha signed.

Sara scrunched her fingers in front of her face. *She's angry.*

"Upset, that's for sure," Keesha replied. She waited until Sara read her lips.

Sara nodded. "And avoiding us." She ran her index finger down her cheek. "Crying?" Without giving Keesha a chance to answer, she took her by the arm and tugged her down the hall. With only minutes till their next classes they pushed open the bathroom door. Liz Martinson was alone, blowing her nose at the sink. "Time for class," she said.

Sara nodded. *"In a minute. I'm sorry*

about yesterday. Still upset? I don't under-
stand. Is it the bridge?"

School.

Radley Academy? This school?

Yes. Liz took another tissue. "I'm probably leaving. My parents think I should withdraw now. According to my father we might be having 'serious financial setbacks.'"

"They wouldn't make you leave! What about a scholarship?"

"With my grades? I'm not smart enough like you two. Plus we make too much money for financial aid. At least Dad used to. They've already talked to the school. They've already talked to everybody but me. I'm the only one in the dark."

Sara stood directly in front of her friend to make sure she understood every word. Twice she asked Liz to slow down.

"My parents have had to hire a lawyer. They're worried about the expense. My sister's in college, so I'm the first one who'll lose tuition." Tears welled in Liz's eyes again. "We had a terrible fight. I said they could cancel the stupid riverboat party to keep me in school."

"Pretty drastic," Keesha said.

"Pretty dumb, too. Everything's already been ordered and contracts have been signed. Besides, school's a lot more expensive than the party."

Sara tried to get back to the problem. "Lawyer?"

"Some hotshot from Pittsburgh."

"Your father's company — engineers, contracts. He must use lawyers all the time."

"This time it's for himself. Maybe even for us."

Sara signed *Why?*

I don't know much, Liz signed. "Sunday morning he and Mom were in the kitchen talking about the bridge. Problems with the Shadow Point Bridge is all he'd tell me." *Problems with the bridge.*

Sara nodded that she was following the conversation.

"Dad says not to worry. These things aren't my concern. Meanwhile he's turning my whole life upside down. Something's really wrong. That's all I know. I tried to forget about it and the next thing I know you're dragging me right to the bridge on bikes yesterday."

Sara circled her heart. "I didn't know."

"I can tell by looking at Dad that my whole life's about to change." Liz picked up her books. "And to make matters worse, I can tell that *his* whole life's about to change, too."

Chapter 7

Sara's school day at Radley Academy was so demanding and took so much concentration, it forced her to forget everything but the subject at hand and the information Mrs. Andrews' fingers gave her in each class. She didn't see Liz again until dismissal when they joined the rest of the crew team at the school van in the parking lot.

As usual the coach drove them the few miles to the Tenth Street Bridge and over to Shelter Island and the boathouse. As they crossed the Buckeye, Sara wondered if every bridge was a bitter reminder to Liz.

The boathouses were busy. Students from half a dozen schools and colleges were in the workout rooms rowing in place on the ergometers. The rest carried their narrow rowing shells down to the waterside platforms or back into the boathouses where they were stored on racks, one above the other.

The coach put the Radley team through their exercises, then a jog along the tree-lined, waterside trail that rimmed the island.

"I'm so frustrated and angry, I'm going to take it out on the water," Liz panted to Sara as they returned to the boathouse.

Sara patted Liz's shoulder and gave her a thumbs-up gesture.

The rowing was exhausting, but the air was clear and the exercise felt good. For the first time all day, Sara was focused. Speed and teamwork drove everything else from her head. Liz, too, was rowing as if nothing else mattered.

Their shell skimmed the water as they pulled together, letting heavy undergrowth that hugged the shore glide by them. Sara kept the rhythm in her head and watched the afternoon sunlight glint off the wake as it widened and drifted out behind them. Ahead at the bend in the river, Radley's cityscape loomed along the banks. In the distance a tugboat pushed a coal barge toward the commercial docks.

At the end of the practice, they turned their shell around and headed back for the docking platform. The current was slow and half a dozen ducks drifted at the shoreline.

As they arrived Sara sank her head onto her oar to catch her breath. Even with her eyes closed, dread tightened the skin under her T-shirt. She raised her head. The photographer from that morning was standing among the trees that lined the bank.

Most of the photographer's face was obscured under a baseball cap, but she could see the determined set of his jaw and the thin, gray trail of cigarette smoke. He aimed and shot, aimed and shot. As he put his camera in his shoulderbag, another man appeared at his shoulder and spoke to him. The photographer nodded and turned to leave.

Sara sank her head back on the oar. The city was proud of its recreational waterfront and sponsored the Buckeye regatta every October. Rowing shells in the afternoon light made spectacular photographs and posters; she had one in her bedroom. The photographer had seen crossed oars on her jacket that morning; maybe he'd simply decided to follow up at the river that afternoon. Lots of rowers; great shots. Maybe none of it had anything to do with her.

Her coach signaled for the team to get out of the shell. Sara's reverie distracted her and she rocked precariously on her narrow seat before following the others as they clambered onto the dock. She forced herself to concentrate as they bent to lift the boat from the water. The photographer drifted from view.

Sara hefted the shell up and over her head with the others and tried to convince herself the man was an ordinary newspaper photographer. She hoped he'd at least gotten some strong action shots of the boat. Maybe he'd caught Liz and it would make the morning paper. That might help convince Liz's parents that she needed to stay at school. The shell was heavy and easily tipped, which forced Sara to concentrate on moving it over her head and up the ramp into its cradle at the back of the boathouse. When she came back into the daylight the photographer was gone.

* * *

Steve was asleep when Sara returned to their apartment. She ate dinner alone and wondered how many meals would be like this, and how long it would take to get used to it. They needed to go over a shopping list. As her guardian, he had to sign a permission slip for a biology field trip. She just needed company. When her brother finally appeared, Sara was in the den finishing an English reading assignment.

He blinked the light in greeting and came in with a plate of leftovers. "Interrupting?"

She shook her head and waved him in. "You're lucky you didn't find me dead of fright when you got back this morning," she said as she told him about her visit from Brenda Fletcher.

Steve circled his heart. "I wanted to make sure you would be okay." When he'd apologized, he put his dinner on the coffee table and sat up straight, elbows on his knees. She read his posture. He wanted her to be able to read his lips and understand. He started slowly. *"School still tough?"*

I'm getting used to it.

Sara closed her book. They talked about

groceries. After he signed the field trip paper, she leaned back. "You wrote *Adam Street* on the mirror last night. Is that why they called you to work? Are you on a new case?"

"Did I forget to wipe that off?" He tried to cover his surprise with a bite of dinner.

"It was dark last night. Were you out there alone?"

"It's dark every night. You mustn't worry, Sara, even when my work's confidential."

I understand you won't tell me anything about it.

Can't.

Or won't, she repeated to herself. She searched for a change of subject. *Liz might have to leave school. Money problems at home.*

Steve averted his eyes and spoke as he stabbed a piece of potato.

Sara jabbed her thumb up to indicate that he needed to face her.

He still looked uncomfortable. "Did she say why she has money problems?"

Sara shrugged to show that she didn't know.

Steve straightened up. *Never mind for now. I have big news. Surprise for you.*

Sara tapped her chest.

Steve nodded and spoke as he worked at signing. *"I booked a weekend at Hidden Acres."* He pointed to her and continued with his hands. *You, me. No work. No interruptions. We can talk about school . . .* He shrugged to show that he didn't know the signs. "We can talk about how things are going for you. How I can help more."

"And you'll tell me about Adam Street?" Sara asked and signed.

"Sara, don't worry about my work."

"Sorry."

"We will talk. I promise. Time away. Keeping my job going, getting on with my life, taking care of you . . ." He fumbled with his hands. "I'm not doing the best job of being your guardian. I'm out at night . . . distracted."

"You're fine. You don't need to be so protective. You can relax."

We will relax. You bring a friend. Bike trails, pool's still open. Great food.

She was bolstered by his mood, and a wave of affection for all his effort washed over her. *"Thanks! We need it, Steve. I have things I want to tell you. You're always at work or I'm at school. This would be a good chance. I'd like to get away this weekend."*

Steve shook his head and finger spelled thirty.

The thirtieth! Sara put her hands up in dismay. *No thirtieth. The Martinsons' party on the* Buckeye Queen *is the thirtieth.*

"This is more what you like to do. Bring people you want."

"I can bring anybody I want to the party, too."

"No Buckeye Queen, *Sara."*

Why? Her disappointment changed to alarm. Steve's insistence was written all over him. She wished he'd lean back into the chair or cross his legs. He seemed almost formal and his mouth was hardly more than a tight line. She studied his eyes. *"It's my friend's party. Good for me to make friends. I can't go to Hidden Acres."*

"Liz isn't like you, Sara."

Say again.

Different, Steve signed. "The Martinsons are in a different social class. They're too wealthy for you. You can't keep up with Liz. This friendship will only hurt you."

"Money! Liz doesn't care whether I have money." She stared at her brother, not bothering to mask her alarm. Something was wrong. He was dismissing Liz the same way he had when she'd tried to tell him about the cemetery and the bridge. She signed and spoke, too, to make sure he understood. *"Liz needs me. Especially right now. If I don't go to her party, she'll think I don't care about her problems."*

Not your problems. "You can find out what's bothering her without going to the party. Bring Keesha for the weekend."

"Keesha's going to the party. So am I."

"I want you away for the weekend." Steve's fingers flew.

Sara choked on her anger and stopped speaking. *You can't just boss me around. You're not Dad. Dad would never have done this!*

Pain played across Steve's face. He sank

back into the chair and ran his hand through his sandy-colored hair. "I hate that he's gone, hate it as much as you do, but I'm in charge now. Dad would have said the same thing. Maybe you'd be just as angry at him."

Never! She stood and turned her back.

Steve got to his feet and turned her back around. "Don't use your deafness against me. It's frustrating enough. I have to concentrate on everything you say. I miss half of what you sign. I hate your deafness. If you could hear me, I wouldn't have to worry so much. You'd understand what I'm trying to — " He winced and circled his heart. *Sorry.* He touched her arms, but she shook him off. "I didn't mean that the way it sounded."

"Sounded? *I can't hear, remember?*" Tears were in Sara's eyes.

Sorry. Sorry. Sorry.

"*Then think about how I feel. What's really wrong?*"

"*Don't know what you mean,*" Steve signed and said.

Yes you do! "*My invitation's been on the refrigerator for a week. It's a big party. It'll help me fit in with the kids at school. I'm deaf, Steve. D-E-A-F. I need the party.*" She could tell by his expression that he didn't understand. She spoke. "You knew all about it and you never forget dates. There's more going on. *Something about the bridge?*" When he flushed, she leaned forward. "*What's going on with the bridge? Why is Mr. Martinson in trouble?*"

Not your worry, he signed and stood up. "I'm your guardian. Sometimes I have to do what's best."

She gave him her best blank stare. *Too much blushing when you're hiding something. First the file. Then Adam Street. Now Liz.*

"It isn't Liz."

"You just said it was Liz." *Too rich. Too fancy.*

"After all you've been through, I wanted us to get away. From Radley . . . from everything. I'll call the Martinsons myself if you'll feel better," Steve said firmly.

Feel better! She was glad to see him wince again.

"Blame it on me, Sara, but tell Liz you

can't go. I'm responsible for you and that's my decision."

Don't ever think you can replace Dad.

Steve closed his eyes in pain, the only indication that he'd understood. Without replying, he took his dinner and went back into the kitchen.

Chapter 8

Sara rubbed her temples against the onslaught of a headache. Steve's signing wasn't fluent and his temper got in the way as much as hers. She was hurt and she'd hurt him. Maybe she'd misunderstood. All they had was each other and maybe Steve was just trying too hard to protect her. She knew Liz Martinson had more money and social standing as well as she knew Keesha Fletcher was African-American. None of it made any difference to any of them. None of it had ever mattered to her father. None of it had ever mattered to Steve.

Her throat tightened. It hadn't been like this before. Before. At Edgewood she never misunderstood anybody. No one was secretive or overbearing. Life in the cloistered school community was trouble free, smooth. Steve had been the cute, distant big brother, back in Radley with Dad. When she'd been at home with her father and brother it was always vacation time, fun, adventure. She'd never had to analyze what Steve said — or why he said it. He'd never been in charge of anything more than driving her to a movie or across the city. She swiped angrily at a tear. Everything had changed. She felt as though she were swimming underwater. She ached for Edgewood, her deaf friends, her support.

Steve was still in the kitchen, poking at his dinner with the fork when Sara entered, notebook in hand. He looked up, his mouth set in a thin line. She waited for him to circle his heart, but there was no apology. She tapped her binder and signed *Keesha*.

Steve signed *Police station*.

She shrugged to show that she didn't care.

Sara did care. Another night alone, this one full of tension and unanswered questions. She left the apartment aching, more frustrated than ever. Their shorthand had always been a language in itself. As kids they'd understood each other with hardly more than a gesture. Why couldn't things always be as clear and simple?

Before Sara knocked on the Fletchers' door across the hall, she leaned against the wall and closed her eyes. She did have studying to do, even if it was not the kind her brother suspected. She thought about Steve's glance, his clear, blue eyes and the worry in them. Something about the bridge? Something about the Martinsons?

Alone in the hall, she signed the worst expletive she could think of. How could Steve think he could concoct a coincidence that would keep her from the riverboat party? Sara crossed the hall. She intended to study some more facial expressions. If she couldn't get answers from Steve, she'd search for them elsewhere.

Keesha's father, John Fletcher, was foreman for West End Construction Company. Although they hadn't gotten the job, Keesha had told her that West End had been one of the companies that bid on repairing the Shadow Point Bridge.

Mr. Fletcher answered the buzzer and immediately looked apologetic. "Marcus just drove Keesha to the store. Out of graph paper for homework."

Sara nodded that she understood and pointed to him. "Question. For you."

"Me? Then come on in." He continued to speak as he turned and led her to the kitchen. At the door he turned back around. "I'm sorry. I forgot you need to read my lips." This time he smiled and looked directly at her. "Come in."

Mrs. Fletcher was at her desk in the alcove they used for a home office. She was surrounded by shelves that held everything from her collection of children's literature to John Fletcher's engineering and construction manuals.

Brenda Fletcher signed, *Hi,* then held up her mug. "Cocoa?"

Sara shook her head. "Project for science. Bridge construction. Different kinds of designs." She hoped the twinges of guilt weren't giving her away as she waited until John Fletcher nodded that he'd understood.

"What can happen to weaken trusses underneath the structure? What could make the girders snap?" She took a breath. "Like Shadow Point Bridge."

Keesha's father arched his eyebrows and glanced at his wife. As inconspicuously as possible, Sara studied Brenda Fletcher's lips. "Be careful. All you've heard are rumors. No charges," Keesha's mother said.

No charges! Sara's pulse raced. Mr. Fletcher's demeanor had changed from cheerful to wary. He tapped the table with his index finger. "Sara." He glanced quickly back to his wife. "Would it be possible to choose another subject?"

Had she understood? "Not the bridge?"

He nodded.

"Could be any bridge," Sara said.

"I know, but . . ." After one more glance at his wife, he sighed. When he spoke it was slow and deliberate. "You and Keesha are best friends with Liz Martinson."

Sara nodded.

"Any bridge project might be too close to home."

Sara frowned. "House?" *Say again.*

"Too close to *home* — an expression." He

pulled a scrap of paper from his wife's desk and wrote: *No bridge. Pick another subject.*

Sara's pulse stayed quick. "Why?"

John Fletcher chewed his lip. "Problems."

"Of course. I know. Accident. Collapsed."

"More than that. This week . . . the company that repaired the damage has found some" — he looked as uncomfortable as she'd ever seen him — "problems."

"With the bridge?"

"Yes. Things not built right. Materials not up to code. Some structural engineers suspect it was done on purpose to save money. There's going to be an investigation of Patrick Martinson's company because of shoddy construction."

Sara watched his mouth but frowned. *Say again.*

"Sloppy work."

"Liz's father did sloppy work? On purpose?" Sara was astounded.

John Fletcher tapped his chest. "I don't think so."

"But others do?" Sara demanded.

"Yes."

Sara's shoulders slumped. She'd read enough mysteries and seen enough movies to know that "on purpose" could mean payoffs, kickbacks, and major scandals. Five people had died in the collapse. Her hands turned clammy. Sloppy work could also mean manslaughter. Prison. In her mind's eye she didn't see the bridge or the rubble, she saw Steve, flushed, evasive, trying to drag her out of town on the thirtieth because he didn't want her to associate with Liz. How many other parents would feel the same way once the story broke?

"I'll pick another topic," she said as she nodded numbly that she understood. In fact she was beginning to understand everything.

She hated being in her apartment by herself. Long after she'd returned, Sara sat at the desk in her bedroom. Steve had kept his word and gone to the station. She had a chapter to read for English. It was almost ten and the words kept swimming in front of her.

She felt even worse about the bike trip. No wonder Liz had been so upset at the bridge.

No wonder her father had to hire an attorney. Liz's life was falling apart and it had to do with a whole lot more than leaving school. For all Sara knew, at that moment she had more information about the scandal than Liz did.

Poke around some more. She signed her father's message to herself and thought about his doodles. She wasn't a little kid and she wasn't stupid. Steve couldn't protect her from news that would shake the city as soon as the press got wind of it.

She closed her book and stared at the rowing poster as Tuck nudged her, ready for his bedtime walk around the block. Sara got up and motioned for the dog to follow her, but stopped at the den and snapped on the light. Her father's manila folder still was where Steve had dropped it in the wastebasket. She pulled it out to study the simple message one more time. The file folder was empty! No message; no doodles. She searched the basket carefully. Her balled-up math homework was still there along with two candy wrappers, and the previous week's television guide. Her pulse jumped. Everything was untouched with one exception. The notes from inside the file were missing.

Steve had pretended it was nothing, but he'd taken them. Tuck nudged her. Suddenly she didn't want to go out. She wanted company, reassurance. She rubbed her arm against the chills, then reluctantly snapped Tuck into his leash.

The elevator was empty; the street deserted. Traffic was light. She tried to ignore the shadows. Awnings, window boxes, an alley entrance became silhouettes of bridges, crouching photographers, well-meaning neighbors. She urged Tuck to a trot. Home, bed, answers. She raced him back to the lobby.

She was lost in thought as she took the elevator to the seventh floor. As the doors slid back and Tuck trotted ahead of her, a shadow swayed at the far end of her hall. A figure passed her door, then the Fletchers'. He crossed the carpet to the staircase marked EXIT and disappeared through the heavy metal fire door.

Tuck's tail wagged. She forced herself to dismiss it, but wrinkled her nose as she unlocked her apartment. Whoever had been there smoked heavily. She shook her head and silently scolded herself. Stop it, Sara! It was just someone who had been visiting and who felt like walking down the stairs.

Chapter 9

The walk to school the next day was uneventful. *No photographer,* Sara signed to Keesha as she passed the townhouse from the day before. Keesha spent half the time walking backwards so she could understand every word and gesture. Sara's backpack straps dug into her shoulders as she kept her hands free and explained everything.

"Was he one of the photojournalists Mom kicked out of the lobby when your dad died? There must have been dozens, even at the funeral," Keesha said.

Probably. Pest.

Right.

Sara moved on to the fabricated science

assignment she'd used to bring up the subject of the bridge with Keesha's father.

"Dad hasn't said a thing to me!" Keesha said indignantly.

He wants to keep it quiet, Sara explained.

Quiet. "What about the newspaper? Something this big is bound to make the *Gazette.* Front page, too."

Say again, Sara signed.

Front page, Keesha repeated with her fingers.

"It gets worse." *Worse. My stupid brother.*

Keesha signed *S, brother,* their name sign for *Steve.*

Sara nodded. "Doesn't want me to go to the riverboat party. Doesn't want me to be friends with Liz anymore. He tried to make me think it was because they have more money. *Now I know the real reason. Patrick Martinson's under police investigation.*"

Keesha was quiet for the last half a block. When they'd crossed the last intersection she turned to face her friend again. "Don't be too hard on Steve. Maybe he's on the case. If there was illegal stuff done to the bridge and people died . . ." She looked away before she glanced back. "Sara, maybe Steve's on the case and he'll have to arrest Liz's father."

Sara put her hand to her stomach as if she'd been punched and shook her head angrily. They'd reached the campus and other students milling around before the late bell. Sara purposely replied with just her hands. *Police work is separate from me. Dad kept it that way and so will Steve. I can't desert Liz just because her father got into trouble. Bad friend.*

Good friend. Best friend, Keesha added.

Thanks. I want Liz to think so, too.

But Steve's your brother. Sara smiled but her stomach was doing flip-flops. This mess might be the kind of thing that hard-nosed detectives didn't understand, but family should, and Steve was all the close family she had.

That afternoon she put all her energy into rowing, but the minute crew was over and the van had returned them to school, Sara gathered her book bag and headed for familiar territory. She entered Radley's Penn Street police precinct headquarters just before six o'clock. She and her brother were like ships in the night. At the moment that was fine. She was still too angry and frustrated to want to see him. According to the schedule he'd kept all week, he'd still be at home, maybe even trying to pull a dinner together they could eat in separate rooms — and a separate room was just where she wanted him.

Although she was as comfortable at the station as in her own apartment, the calming influence of a normal school day and good rowing practice had drained away. Anxiety knotted her stomach as she thought of what she was after.

The small city building was a combination garage and office and sat at the corner of Penn and Harrison, the streets that divided the residential area from the shopping district. Sara inhaled the warm smell of chocolate from the Buckeye Foods bakery and waved at the two rookies who were standing by their squad car. No Steve so far.

The desk officer was at the computer with his back to the bulletin board, a collage of posted announcements, community information, and the latest wanted posters, local and national. She didn't stop to read any of it. Next to it was a framed, formal photograph of her father. While he hadn't died in the line of duty, Paul Howell had been a revered member of the Radley detective squad since his first days on the force. Even after he'd been transferred to headquarters, this was the station he'd visit, with Sara tagging along.

When Steve had been assigned to the fourth precinct he called it old home week. How much happier they all were back then. She looked at the photograph and signed, *Forgive me Dad* as she slipped past the desk sergeant and up the staircase.

She took the stairs two at a time and followed the narrow hall that led to a warren of brightly lit spaces. The door to the interrogation room was closed. The office Steve shared with two other detectives who rotated their shifts was open and empty. It was small, with an open window that overlooked the row houses along Penn Street. She laid her book bag on the floor and sat in Steve's chair.

She watched the pattern of dusky light from the maple tree while she gathered her courage, then scanned the chaos on her brother's desk. Beside the phone was a group of framed photos: their mother grinning at Paul Howell then a handsome rookie in uniform right out of the police academy. There was a small one of Steve in uniform with their father beside him. Next to it was last year's school photo of her at Edgewood. The reminder that her brother kept her picture on his desk added to her guilt.

Her hand hovered over the scramble of notes, morning paper, and manuals all under impromptu paperweights. She hardly dared to touch them, let alone rearrange anything. She sucked in a deep breath and moved the *Gazette*. A fresh file folder caught her eye, half buried under a stack of forms. Instead of the usual white file label, this folder read *Dad* in black permanent marker.

Poke around some more. She pressed her fist against the butterflies in her stomach. What could it hurt? Steve had left the file in plain sight. She reached for it as if it were hot, then froze as a hand clamped on her shoulder.

Sara spun in the chair. Lt. Rosemary

Marino pushed her fingers forward and flipped her pinky in the H-I movement which meant *Hi.*

Hi, was all Sara could manage.

The community liaison officer had worked with her father on developing drug information for the Radley schools and had a wall of awards for her undercover work. She was also the only one who attempted to sign.

Sara tried to recover. "I know Steve's not here. I just thought . . ."

Officer Marino nodded toward the hall. "Steve is here."

Sara's heart sank.

"Your brother's in a meeting in the interrogation room. He shouldn't be too long."

"In a meeting?"

Lt. Marino nodded. "Aren't you looking for him?"

Deafness had its advantages. Sara smiled but made no more attempt to communicate. Lt. Marino smiled back and left the room. Sara spun around a second time in her brother's chair. Without a moment to lose, she pulled the folder by a corner until it was free. Perspiration dampened her palms. She looked at the doorway, out the window, then back to the desk.

Chills started up her back as the breeze rose. Leaves danced on the branch closest to the sill and warm, chocolate-smelling air wrapped around her.

The file was so thin she thought it might have been empty. She opened it. *Poke around some more* and the doodles lay on top of half a dozen pieces of scrap paper and notecards. She'd hit pay dirt, but something close to fright kept her palms damp. She stared at her father's handwriting. She stared at the door. Her deafness blocked footsteps, voices, the creak of a door. Her only hope of not being caught a second time was shadows, glimpses of her brother's silhouette as he came down the hall from his meeting.

Doorway to desk, doorway to desk. She switched her glance from one to the other a dozen times as she skimmed the notes Steve had added to the file. For the moment she forgot about Martinson Engineering and the bridge. Whatever Steve knew had compelled him to build on her father's knowledge.

There was nothing on the papers to indicate what it might be except Adam Street, the same words Steve had scrawled on the bathroom mirror, and two phone numbers scribbled without any other notation. She wrote them down. The sheet with her father's doodles was there, arches and curves and parallel lines as though he'd doodled absently while talking on the phone or running something over in his mind. Steve had added something equally confusing. TILLMAN AND REED'S BOOK, in his familiar block letters, was printed at the top of the page.

As she copied it all into her homework assignment pad, wind lifted the scraps. The sheet danced under her flat hand. She blew a strand of hair off her eyebrow, closed the file, and grabbed her backpack. She wanted out. This was not the place to try and make sense of what her brother was up to.

As she got up, movement caught her eye. The precinct lieutenant and two patrol officers walked past the open door. She put her hand back against the butterflies, but managed to open the *Radley Gazette*. She looked for the photos from rowing practice or her walk to school in the crew jacket. There were none.

Steve entered the room before she could do more than sink back into his chair. He poked the newsprint. She put down the paper and looked up at him, all innocence, and found his usual scrutiny. It was a long, hard look and it made her blush.

Guilty! he signed with the start of a smile.

I don't know what you mean.

You're blushing. He brushed his cheeks. *I bet you're here to apologize.*

Am not! She frowned and hoped she looked indignant.

Steve sat on the edge of his desk. "Then I will. I'm glad you stopped by. We have to start somewhere. I'm sorry about yesterday. I went about things wrong. I still need practice being a parent, but you have to trust me. I never, never meant to hurt you about being deaf. I love you just the way you are." He poked his chest. *It's me. I'm frustrated.*

"You're talking instead of signing on purpose."

Steve smiled innocently.

She scowled. One of the worst things about being deaf was the necessity of looking right at the speaker to read lips. It was impossible to turn an angry shoulder without blocking out all speech, as she had the night before. She didn't want a rehash of that. She crossed her arms over her chest, already anticipating the clenched jaw, the frown, the thin, stern line of his mouth. Steve Howell could be the most irritating combination of mother, father, guardian, cop.

He was dressed in jeans and an oxford shirt and while she scowled he worked at a loose button on his cuff. *You go first,* he signed. *You came all the way over here to tell me something. Right?*

He didn't know how wrong he was, but she wasn't about to confess that she was here to go through his files. Instead she let her fingers fly. *Stop being so suspicious of everything in my life. Don't start choosing my friends. I hardly have any as it is and now you won't let me go to Liz's party where everybody'll be. It's hard Steve, hard being the only deaf kid at school. Hard being different. Nobody knows how to treat me yet, nobody but Liz and Keesha. Let me go to the party. Everybody'll see I can be just like them. They'll see me outside school. They'll see I'm normal.*

Steve looked stricken and pulled her into a hug. When he let her go he sighed. "So much to think about. I didn't know school was that hard for you."

"Adjustment. Understand?"

Yes. "You can't blame me for being concerned." He circled his heart. *Sorry.*

Me too. You're making an okay father.

Thanks.

Then I can go?

I don't know. Some things are for your own good. He cupped her chin. "If I don't do a good job of caring for you, our grandparents will ship you back to Edgewood. Every school vacation will be with them at their retirement homes. Don't you know I think about that all the time?"

She didn't have the heart to tell him how often she thought about Edgewood — and never as punishment.

Chapter 10

Good job, Sara signed, finally, reluctantly. Despite her anger and frustration, Steve's anguish made her relax. She did need to stop and remind herself how hard he tried, how responsible he felt. She just wished it didn't feel as though she were being smothered. *I'm safe, Steve.*

I want to keep you that way.

Trust me? Trust my judgment?

Yes. Of course.

Let me go to Liz's party. She needs me right now. I know about the mess with her dad. Mr. Fletcher told me last night. You knew and didn't tell me. That's why I'm here, she fibbed.

It was Steve's turn to blush. He nodded.

You wouldn't desert a friend and neither will I.

"There's more to this than you know," Steve said.

"Are you working on the case?"

Steve sighed. "No." He looked at her skeptical expression. "That's the truth. They're working on it at headquarters, downtown. It's not my case, not even this precinct's case."

"Then you won't have to . . ." Her throat constricted and she changed to sign . . . *arrest Mr. Martinson — if they find — whatever they're looking for?* She could barely get the words out, even with her fingers.

Steve put his arm around her shoulder. "If it makes you feel better, no, Sara, it won't be me."

She signed. *Liz needs me at her party as much as I need to go.* She wished she could read her brother's mind, jump into his head and make sense of what he knew.

I'll think it over.

Sara hugged him. It felt good and it was a start.

* * *

She left Steve at the police station and wolfed down dinner. She had a legitimate excuse to cross the hall to the Fletchers. She needed to choose an author for her English assignment on children's books and Mrs. Fletcher had them all. Brenda Fletcher answered the door on her way out to a school meeting.

Marcus and his father were in the living room with a stack of college catalogues in front of them. Sara settled with Keesha in the office alcove off the kitchen.

Keesha pointed to her mother's collection, but Sara shook her head and impatiently pulled the scrap of paper from her pocket. She sat down at the desk and tugged Keesha into the chair next to her. She smiled at her friend's curious expression.

"What are you up to, Sara?"

"I don't know." She put her fingers against Keesha's mouth. *Sign from now on.*

Keesha automatically glanced in the direction of the living room. "What's up?" *What's the matter?*

Sara handed her the slip of paper.

Some hot guys' numbers?

Sara grinned but shrugged. *No idea.*

As simply as possible Sara explained what she'd found in her brother's office and where she'd found it. *Unless I go through the relay operator or these lines have TTYs, I can't —*

Hold on! You want me to play detective? Keesha tapped her chest. *What if your dad was working on something really dangerous? Obviously the case wasn't closed or Steve wouldn't be interested. Sara, your brother will go through the roof.* She raised her hand in the direction of the ceiling. *Why is this so important? Why not just ask Steve why he took the file and added to it?*

Sheepishly Sara shrugged and repeated the through-the-roof gesture. *I can't tell him I snooped and found it in his office, especially after he insisted it wasn't even a file worth keeping. Besides, I got enough confidential information out of him today. He's not working on the Martinson case.*

Great. That must be a relief. But you want me to be an accomplice to find out about the rest?

Do you have a map of Radley?

That must mean yes. Keesha opened a

desk drawer and pulled out a city map. Sara thumbed to the index and scanned for Adam Street. There was Acorn, Adair Avenue, Addison Lane, and Allegheny Boulevard. No Adam. She turned to the phone numbers.

Keesha frowned. *It's after eight. If these are business numbers we should wait till normal working hours.*

Try one. You're my best friend.

Keesha shook her head but picked up the phone and tapped out the first number. Sara stared as she tried to read her friend's expression. Keesha's lips didn't move, but she nodded, then hung up.

Tape message. The recording says it's the county courthouse. The message said to call back during normal working hours unless you want night court. She scribbled on a piece of paper and slid it to Sara. *Steve goes there all the time, right?*

Sara reluctantly nodded. *Could be anything. Lawyer's office. A judge's office. Steve testifies in court cases. All kinds of offices are there.*

Keesha frowned. "Read my lips. I'm not

making any noise but I don't know the signs."

Sara nodded.

"All I got was the main switchboard. Didn't Steve write down an extension number? We could call that in the morning and at least find out what department he was interested in."

Sara shook her head.

Keesha glanced toward the living room. *I better start talking a little or Dad'll think I'm up to something. We hardly ever sign completely. Maybe you better pick out the books for your project.*

Sara agreed and stood up to scan the shelf that held Mrs. Fletcher's collection. She was so distracted the titles swam in front of her. She pointed to the second phone number. Keesha picked up the receiver again, but Sara pushed her arm down. She grabbed the Radley phone book and hastily paged through it on a hunch she hoped would be wrong. She ran her finger down the long column until she came to Martinson Engineering Co. The number matched the one she had copied from Steve's notes.

Keesha followed her finger and shook her head. *You just told me Steve wasn't working on the Martinson case.* Comprehension widened her eyes. *All these numbers have to do with the Shadow Point Bridge?*

Sara tapped Keesha's arm. *Steve has all these numbers under DAD, my father's file.*

There was no need to sign or say what they both realized. Steve Howell had discovered that his father had been working on something to do with the bridge. *Poke around some more.* A dusty folder on a bottom shelf. Sara's anxiety turned to chills.

As usual Steve was out overnight. Sara roamed around the apartment with Tuck. Part of her ached for her brother to be there, but it was easier this way. *Steve, I just happened to be going through the information you added to Dad's file, the one you told me wasn't a file at all and meant nothing. The one I took off your desk at the police station. I was wondering why you had the phone number of the courthouse on an index card, and, by the way, who are Tillman and Reed?*

Steve wouldn't even bother to send her

back to Edgewood. He'd pack her off to one set of grandparents before she could grab a suitcase. Lucky to be a dog, she thought as she looked at Tuck. She was bursting with questions she knew she couldn't ask. Questions Steve wouldn't answer. At ten o'clock she convinced Keesha to walk Tuck with her.

Before finally settling into a restless sleep, Sara lay in bed and thought about her brother and where he might be that night. Part of her was afraid for him, the way she had been for her father, the part that Lt. Howell had never been able to reassure, no matter how hard he'd tried.

Though her father never said it, sending her to Edgewood had to do with more than her education. She loved the school, loved being immersed in a deaf community, but Edgewood School for the Deaf had also kept her removed from the daily suspense of her father's police work. There was nothing to keep her from the danger and intrigue in Steve's life except his silence and her ignorance.

* * *

She slept with her bedroom door open and the lamp in the foyer on. Always on. Light played along her walls as traffic moved outside. Unconsciously she reached over the edge of the bed for Tuck and ruffled his ears.

Maybe Adam Street led to the offices of Martinson Engineering. Right now detectives were working to prove criminal intent in the construction of a bridge. Negligence seemed serious enough. Her father must have known or suspected it. She closed her eyes; she was back on the trail that led to the scene of the accident. She punched her pillow and wished she'd never looked at the file.

Chapter 11

There was no time to waste. At lunch Sara told her rowing coach she had to skip practice to do library research. As long as Coach Barns didn't ask what the research was for, it wasn't really a lie. Only Keesha knew what she had in mind.

While Liz and the others dressed for practice, Sara gathered her books into her backpack. Although clouds were forming, rain wasn't predicted till evening and as the team hustled out to the van, she left through the gym entrance and crossed the street to the bus stop. As she leaned against the telephone pole, she absently scanned the line of cars parked along the city curb. She stopped and squinted at a navy blue sedan close to the end of the block. It was one of the unmarked police cars from Steve's precinct. She knew them all.

Sara squinted at the person behind the wheel. Lt. Marino was sipping a cup of coffee. Sara knew better than to wave or call attention to her. Two students had their car stereos stolen during school hours and the officer might very well be working on a stakeout, or something even more serious. Sara turned away as the Radley city bus lumbered between them and stopped. Once she climbed the steps and paid her fare, all she could see was the hood of the car.

The Radley Free Library faced Penn Square at the end of Harrison Street and helped to frame the city park. Despite modernization, the building was still full of wood and brass and dim reading lamps. The atmosphere had become all the more interesting in June when she'd asked a great-looking summer employee for help. Bret Sanderson had introduced himself in ASL and explained that although his hearing was normal, he had deaf parents. They joked that they were the only ones who could converse freely in the library without being hushed by someone else in charge.

She'd told him she'd stop by at the end of the summer between camp and her return to Edgewood. *Before my life fell apart,* she thought now as she climbed the library steps. She hadn't been back. June seemed years ago.

Sara put her backpack onto the reference desk and spoke carefully to the woman in charge. "I need back issues of the *Radley Gazette.*"

The librarian pointed to the room behind her.

As Sara slung her backpack over her shoulder, she turned a corner and nearly bumped into Bret, all six feet of him.

His brown eyes widened as he grinned. *Hi, stranger!* he signed, but the smile disappeared. *I'm sorry. I heard about your father.*

Sara signed *Thanks. Still here?*

So far. I work after school till basketball season. When do you go back to your school? Edgewood, was it?

I'm living with my brother. I transferred to Radley Academy.

His grin returned. *I'm at Penham. We play you in most sports. What are you here for? How can I help?*

I need some information. Newspapers. Back issues.

Bret finger spelled *R-A-D-L-E-Y.*

Yes. Back to the collapse of Shadow Point Bridge.

Bret nodded and led her to the bank of computers. *Original coverage of the accident would be in the reference section. Already on microfilm,* he signed as they arrived.

Bret stayed long enough to make sure she found what she was after, then went to help others. Sara was glad he seemed reluctant to go but it was just as well. She read and reread the articles that covered the collapse of the bridge. The first, of course, focused on the tragic loss of life and biographies of the occupants of the cars and truck that had plunged into the Buckeye River. Jazz musicians Karim Jackson and Milo Turnley were crossing the river for an audition. Brian Street had been driving a Shadow Point Marina pickup truck. Elsie Bolling and Margaret

O'Rourke were on their way to a senior citizens' bridge tournament.

By the end of the week, however, the focus had shifted to the bridge itself, the damage, the inspection reports. Sara remembered all too clearly how upset Liz had been. Even though she knew most of the details from badgering her father over her TTY from school, Sara had been relieved to hear from Liz herself. There'd been no hint of scandal or wrongdoing.

Sara scrambled through the index and went back further, through old copies of the newspaper. Four years earlier it wasn't headlines, but it had made the front page. LONG-AWAITED SHADOW POINT BRIDGE OPENS WITH FANFARE.

There was even a photo of Liz with her family. She stood with her sister and mother next to Patrick Martinson as he cut the ribbon. There were city officials, Shadow Point Park's director, even the mayors of Radley and Hillsboro.

Sara continued over the page to the small profile on Patrick Martinson and the award-winning work he'd done as an industrial architectural engineer. There was nothing significant beyond paragraphs on his college degrees and early work for a company in Philadelphia. Sara read it all twice, right through to the last line. **After the company diversified, Patrick Martinson founded his own firm in Radley. With fellow engineer Howard Gillespie, he has specialized in bridge and tunnel construction, combining state-of-the-art technology with award-winning design.**

She rubbed her eyes and shook her head at her naive assumption that something would jump off the page at her.

A hand on her shoulder made her heart leap. *You okay?* Bret smiled. *You look discouraged.*

Sara shook her head. *Just concentrating. Homework project.*

On bridges in general or this one? Bret asked.

General. She could feel her cheeks heat up. White lies were stacking up in her life like pancakes. As she fumbled for conversation that wouldn't bury her deeper, Bret checked his watch and again looked reluctant.

My shift's over. Bus to catch. It'll be nice having you in Radley. Want to do something on the river Saturday? Boat, picnic?

Sara smiled. Did she! She nodded and handed him her phone/TTY number, glad for once that her heart skipped from something other than fear.

Drizzle had started as commuters jammed the bus Sara caught back to her apartment at five o'clock. She held the strap and tried not to think how tempted she'd been to confide in Bret. Those deep brown eyes inspired confidence, and it had been a long time since she'd felt so comfortable with anyone except Keesha. She hardly knew him, but it was a wonderful feeling to find someone in Radley who could speak to her fluently, someone who had his own TTY. Someone she could understand without the constant effort it took to read lips.

As her bus crawled down Harrison Street, she swayed from the strap and tried to think like her father and put the pieces of the puzzle together. A major bridge is built, inspected, opened. Four years later a portion collapses, killing five people. The investigation turns up clean. Tragedy, but no scandal. Members of the victims' families don't sue the city or demand anything. The bridge is rebuilt and reopens. Suddenly, the company that built the bridge is suspected of shoddy construction. All fingers point to the designers and engineers. Patrick Martinson heads the list. There was more — fragments of things she couldn't put into words, thoughts that refused to gel — but none of it made sense.

The apartment was empty, but the kitchen table had been set and dinner started. It smelled deliciously of baked chicken. Home cooking, almost. The delivery bag from Steve's favorite store, Chicken Tonight, was on the counter.

As she changed into jeans and dished out Tuck's dinner, Steve came home with the dog. He hung up the umbrella as Tuck bounded down the hall to her and after a good lick and nuzzle, settled over his filled food and water bowls in the corner.

Sara searched Steve's face for the usual wary expression, then busied herself putting the salads on the table as he served their meal. *Nice to have you home,* she signed and meant it.

He circled his heart. *Work.*

I know. In fact I know more than you can imagine, she wanted to add.

Eating and sign were not compatible, but Steve seemed bent on conversation. Lightning flashed at the window. *Thunder! Rain.*

If practice is rained out tomorrow I'll do the grocery shopping after school.

Thanks. Practice today? He added.

She stared into her potato salad until she was sure no blush would give her away. "Didn't go. I took the bus to the library. Research for school project. The coach gave me the afternoon off."

Steve arched his eyebrows and seemed to chew on her answer as he chewed on his chicken. "What project are you working on?"

She hoped her cheeks wouldn't burn.

"Children's books. Major assignment for English."

Say again.

"Project. Children's books."

"You've told me about the project before. I thought Brenda had the books you needed."

Heat teased her ears as she pretended not to understand. She poked her salad.

Steve tapped her arm so she'd look back at him. "The Fletchers have the books. You shouldn't be wandering around the city."

"Wandering! Penn Square and back. Bus 61C. I've taken that bus all my life." Sara gave him her best shrug. "Mrs. Fletcher has the books, but I needed biographical information. Bret Sanderson, the great-looking librarian who signs, was there. Deaf parents. You met him last June. It was pouring and you came to pick me up. We were signing at the reference desk. We have a date Saturday. River picnic." She put down her fork and signed. *I think he's hot.* She got the reaction she'd hoped for.

Steve grinned and arched his eyebrows. *Great. You and boys. One more thing to worry about.*

Don't worry about boys, or me at the library. Wonderful chicken. When she was sure she'd successfully changed the subject, she got up and served herself from the pan in the oven.

After dinner Steve settled in the living room, but twice before Sara had finished her first homework assignment, he passed down the hall outside her door. Restless. She wished he were thinking about a girl, or a movie, or some latest bestseller, but she knew better. Maybe he'd go out for a jog or down to the athletic club for racquetball.

When he finally did go out, umbrella in hand, it was to walk Tuck one last time. By then Sara had moved into the den with the remains of her history essay. As she dropped her books onto the couch, she glanced at the bookshelf. The old easy chair had been moved and the books on the bottom shelf had been rearranged. She had put *Historic Parks and Gardens Along the Buckeye River* flat, on top of a few others. Now the volumes were lined up, one against the next, so they stuck out from the shelf. She frowned. Steve had been looking for something.

Sara knelt at the edge of the couch and pulled the Radley book back out. The paper clip still marked the section on the Shadow Point Bridge. She looked at it again.

The flowering trees and the fountains, all the attractions the photographer meant to capture, had caught her attention the first time. What she looked at now, however, was the base of the bridge. It was an excellent close-up of the Shadow Point Bridge, an angle someone might want to look at if he or she were interested in the construction. *Poke around some more.* Her father had been following his own advice.

Sara closed the book and went into the kitchen. As she opened the refrigerator, the blinking light of the apartment door buzzer caught her eye. Ten minutes after ten. If Steve had forgotten his key, and was downstairs buzzing to get in, it had been an awfully short walk. She crossed to the foyer, grateful for the peephole in the middle of the door.

Chapter 12

Sara opened the door as Keesha jumped over the threshold. "Is Steve here?"

Out with Tuck. Back soon.

Keesha adjusted her backpack and began to sign. *I was scooping up my books on Mom's desk, it was right on the bookshelf in front of me with Dad's other manuals.*

Sara laughed and pressed her hands over Keesha's. *Slow down! I have no idea what you're talking about.*

Keesha fumbled with her backpack and pulled out a worn textbook. "Look!" *The Evolution of Long Span Bridge Building* trailed down the spine, followed by the names of the authors: *Tillman and Reed*.

Sara's laughter died in her throat. *The last*

names on Steve's notes. Slowly she took the book and flipped through the pages. The doodles she'd found on her father's note matched the architectural renderings of bridge sections. Her father had *not* been randomly scribbling. Here was the proof of what he was working on. She caught her breath and led Keesha to the den. She opened *Historic Parks and Gardens Along the Buckeye River* and laid it flat. When she'd flipped to the photos she'd just been studying, she compared them to the sketches from the text.

My father drew this cross section. Look! The structural core of the same kind of bridge as Shadow Point. Dad knew something was wrong. Maybe not till after the collapse, but something.

What about the rest? What did you find at the library? Keesha looked stricken.

Sara watched her friend finger spell and shook her head. *I ran into a hot guy. B-R-E-T S-A-N-D-E-R-S-O-N works at the library. He signs. He helped me find the articles covering the bridge accident. I read everything. Mr. Martinson started his own firm after working for someone else. He's famous, or at least well-known, respected — or used to be. Wins awards . . . till now.*

Keesha nodded. *If my father already knows about the charges and investigation from his construction connections, you can bet it'll hit the papers any day.*

Sara shuddered as she imagined some reporter chasing Liz's father around with a microphone. "Is it true, Mr. Martinson? . . . A minute of your time, Mr. Martinson? . . ." Too bad he couldn't be deaf: the perfect excuse to ignore them.

Keesha jumped and turned to the door. *Your brother's home. I hear Tuck, too.*

Sara put the garden book away and shoved the engineering manual at Keesha, then signed with shaking fingers. *Tomorrow. Come with me! If there's thunder and lightning we won't row. I'm supposed to go home to get the car and grocery shop, but I want to show you something at the marina first.*

As Steve appeared at the door and said hello, Keesha turned back to Sara and tapped her teeth. "Dentist appointment. Can't."

Steve continued down the hall to his room.

Keesha grabbed Sara by the arm. *You're not doing anything dangerous?*

No. I want to look at the parking lot and marina again, without Liz. Steve swore to me that he's not working on the Martinson case. I don't think he's lying, but you can see he knows Dad knew something about the bridge before he died. Dad might have been starting his own investigation.

And his death is still a mystery. Nobody's come forward; nobody saw anything. You don't suppose — Keesha grimaced and shook her head apologetically.

What?

Nothing. She motioned to the hall and Steve reappeared to say that Keesha was due back across the hall.

It wasn't "nothing." What Keesha had been about to say lurked, even in Sara's head, like a bad dream waiting to be recalled in the morning.

Puddles glistened on the asphalt and her tires kicked up mist as Sara left the Thurston

Court parking garage. She had her father's late-model sedan. Forest green; he'd let her pick the color; she passed her driver's test in it. He'd taken her to dinner to celebrate. Weeks ago she'd reconciled herself to these flashes of memory. How long would it be until they no longer sparked the awful ache behind every rib from her heart to her stomach?

After the accident it had taken Steve three days before he had enough composure to pick up the car and drive it home. She gritted her teeth.

She tapped her fingers impatiently as she worked her way through city traffic to the marina. At the second set of streetlights a familiar black import pulled in two cars behind her.

Kimberly Roth and her car were the envy of the class, and Sara squinted into her rearview mirror for a better view, but couldn't see the driver. She made two turns; the import followed. Sara presumed Kim was on her way to one of the acting or modeling assignments that made her life seem so glamorous, but the car stayed with her to the park entrance. As Sara turned right and into the park, the car continued ahead.

Unlike the weekend, the park was nearly deserted except for employees. The pleasure boats were moored at the piers. A few mechanics and boat owners were scattered among them, but the picnic area and the last tier of the parking lot were empty. The Howells had a medium-sized powerboat — one they all used for fun. Fun. Black Saturday, as she thought of it, her father had been tinkering with the engine before being hit by a car on the way to his own in the back tier of the parking area.

After the accident the marina had offered to haul and store the boat, but she and Steve weren't ready. Sweat broke out on Sara's palms and her hands slid on the steering wheel. She wiped one, then the other on her skirt as she drove toward the park, but nothing helped keep down the anxiety.

She steered the car into the lined space three down from the end, tucked behind the bridge base. The same parking space her father had used. The same car. Sara turned off the ignition and leaned her forehead against the steering wheel. She took deep breaths before finally getting out. Rain threatened and the air was heavy, humid. Like the day of the funeral, she thought.

Her resolve and curiosity had brought her this far but she had no plan. She stood in the empty lot and stared at the car, as if waiting for some imagined wind to come swirling around her. She couldn't think of anything Radley detectives hadn't done a dozen times; nothing Steve hadn't done over and over. There were no clues; no witnesses. Grief stirred and she bit her lip. Not now, she thought. She shielded her eyes and looked up at the silent bridge looming over her, then over into the bike trail.

Tell me what you saw! Let go of your secrets! Her fingers flew. *Here.* She stabbed angrily at the ground. *What happened here?* Frustration tore at her heart and she swiped angrily at the tears blurring her vision. She was through with tears. *Damn bridge! Damn coward murderer wherever you are!*

Her mind was a jumble of facts, speculation, and fears as she looked up at the bridge.

At Edgewood she would lie awake at night and imagine the cases her father and brother were investigating. She'd come up with twists, leads, even solutions. Child's play, she thought, stupid, naive kids' games. They had all come from her imagination.

A Hansel and Gretel trail. The expression popped into her head. It was her father's term when he had only crumbs of information about a case, or a suspect, or even events. He worked the bits and pieces into clues. He'd said to her, "Nine times out of ten, if I'm patient and follow those crumbs, I get a little trail that winds itself through the forest of the crime. If I can just stick with it, bam! I wind up with what I'm after."

Sara closed her eyes. He had been after something Black Saturday. She'd just returned from camp and her father had insisted they all have dinner together. He'd been out, but returned so they could eat early. Then he'd left the apartment to work on the boat. Small repair he had said, something he could finish in the remaining daylight. She remembered him changing into jeans and Steve asking if he needed help. She hadn't bothered to read their lips after that.

Better idea. Her father had changed to signing, the indication that she was included in the conversation. *Why don't the two of you take in the arts festival at city square? I was at the courthouse this afternoon and the festival is set up across the street in the park. Opening night fireworks over the river.*

Steve had said he had plans with his own friends and her father had gone back to speech. She'd caught ". . . time with your sister . . . back to school soon . . ." before both men turned their backs and finished talking.

I'll meet you at the fountain about nine. Family night, her father added. She hadn't wanted to go with Steve any more than Steve had wanted to take her, but they'd agreed because they knew how much it meant to their father. They hadn't met him at the fountain. The police had tracked Steve down through his beeper and at nine o'clock they'd met the ambulance and Paul Howell at the emergency room of East End General Hospital.

* * *

In her head her father's hands flew as he signed. She had no memory of his voice, but his hands and the way he invented signs when he needed an expression were as distinctive as fingerprints. Paul Howell left his own crumbs: the paper-clipped page in the book, the sketches. Now he was dead and scandal was about to break. She pressed her hands to her face against the tears and the isolation that rolled over her like fog off the cliffs at Shadow Point.

Chapter 13

Sara's anger refused to dissipate as she crossed the puddled asphalt to the bridge base. Radley Academy had a strict dress code and she chided herself for not changing out of her skirt, tights, and shoes when she'd gone home for the car. By the time she reached the foundation, the damp had soaked her feet. The saturated shoes would raise blisters if she did much walking.

She was five feet six inches tall, but the bridge foundation dwarfed her. She kicked mud from her ankle and moved into the shelter of the granite block and its landscaped footings, then stared up into the girders.

You have eyes, bridge. Tell me who did it. She waited for the frightening sensation that she was being watched. She tried to call up the gooseflesh she'd felt Sunday when she'd been so sure eyes were on her. Now she looked back up to the infrastructure, into the landscaping, the trail. Nothing.

Answer me! She flattened her hands angrily against the bridge footing and pushed as if she could press an answer out of the rough surface.

Nothing happened; nothing came to her. The damp air barely stirred as it clung. Defeated, she sank her forehead on her arm. Hansel and Gretel trail. Crumbs.

It was a good thing the lot was deserted. Strangers stared at her enough under normal circumstances. Someone was bound to think she had a screw loose. Maybe she did. Maybe she was crazy, but last Sunday something had gotten under her skin enough to signal every fiber of her body.

Sara searched the park. She forced herself to breathe calmly, to think rationally . . . the way Dad was thinking when he was out here, she thought. As Steve is now.

It had been a cloudy Saturday, nearly dusk. Sara glanced back at the car. Certainly the park and marina would have been busy, but many would have left by then. Surely there would have been parking spaces closer to the waterfront.

If her father had intended only a quick boat repair and was due to meet them downtown, it didn't make sense that he would have parked back here, as far away as a car could be from the piers.

"Answers!" Sara thought to herself. She stared at the bridge. Answers weren't here. They were on the trail where it crossed under the bridge, now shrouded in the mist, where her sixth sense had started everything. Her father's file in the den, the notes in Steve's office, the rumors from John Fletcher, the information from the library; she'd found each crumb of her delicate trail since she'd ignored the Shadow Point warning sign and crossed under the bridge Sunday afternoon.

She needed to return. It would be a long, muddy walk by foot from the car back along the bike path to the granite base of the first bridge footing.

With her heart pounding again, she crossed the picnic area to the wooded spot where the

bike trails merged, but she was already slipping in her thin shoes. Moisture seeped over
her toes. She glanced quickly at the empty
parking lot, then ducked under the chain that
closed the bottom of the path.

The hillside trail grew slick with pine needles, dirt, then mud caked her shoes. In some
places the rhododendrons and mountain lau-
rel made navigating nearly impossible. Their
leaves were beaded with rain and each over-
hanging branch might as well have been a
cup holding a final sip. The least budge or
bump sent trickles down her back or on her
hair. She got only as far as the open space at
the second hairpin turn before she started to
slip again. She panted softly as she wiped her
hair from her face and strained for a closer
look.

Without the afternoon sun of Sunday, the
shadows where the trail passed under the
bridge weren't as deep. There was no glare
and she didn't need to squint. Her skin itched
from the wet and as she rubbed her neck, she
caught a patch of blue, nearly the color of
robins' eggs and Sunday's sky. The color of
boat and construction tarps! What she'd mis-

taken for a patch of bright afternoon heaven above the construction tarp on Sunday was still bright against that afternoon's oyster-colored sky. A tarpaulin, propped like a makeshift tent, was tucked nearly back into the point where the bridge met the hillside. Something, somebody was there.

She stumbled and landed on one knee, staining her tights further. Oh, for an ounce of her father's patience. *Think, Sara. Use your head before you use your hands or your feet.* How often had her father signed that to her as she'd struggled to ride a bike, to decipher ASL, to read lips, to drive.

Slow me down, Dad. Patience! She would have sat down and cleared her head while she signed, but it would have only ruined her clothes further. She glanced at her watch and reluctantly made a fist and pulled her thumb out along her chin. Tomorrow. It was too wet and too late to do anything now. Somehow she'd have to summon enough Howell patience to give up temporarily. Steve expected her to arrive any minute with dinner and she hadn't even hit the grocery store. More to the point, there was nothing else she could do on the trail until she had the right clothes and decent sneakers.

She clambered back to the pavement, never taking her eyes off her car and its parking space. Only visible from this side of the bridge, a side closed to the public. If her father had come here to do more sketches of the infrastructure there would have been paper and pencil in the car, or on his body. Maybe he had an appointment that he'd deliberately left out of his date book. Maybe he'd sent Steve with her to keep him away. *Why, Dad*? she signed angrily before losing her footing and putting her arm in the dirt to brace herself.

She drove the car around the perimeter of the parking lot as if giving the park one last chance to reveal its secrets, then to the riverfront and slowly past the marina's machine shop and marine supply store. As she turned to leave the park, she spotted the car that had followed her. It was parked in front of the boat storage shed. Kim might have had a modeling job somewhere at the marina, but when Sara checked quickly for the distinctive KIMZ vanity license, she found only a standard state plate. It hadn't been Kimberly Roth after all.

Of all nights for Steve to be home, Sara would not have chosen this one. She was late with the groceries and blamed it on seeing a teacher after school. She made up a traffic jam for good measure. Her clothes were limp, but she'd stripped off her muddy tights in the elevator on the way up to the apartment and stuffed them into the bottom of a grocery bag until she could get them into the laundry hamper.

They ate dinner in easy silence, almost as if a truce had been called. She ached to tell him what she'd discovered at the marina, to add pieces to his investigation, but, of course, that was impossible. She wasn't supposed to know there was an investigation and she would have had to admit to lying about where she'd spent the afternoon. As they ate she decided if her search turned up anything, she'd tell him then, at a moment when the importance of the information outweighed her deceit.

* * *

More library research. It had worked the first time on Coach Barns, so she tried it again on Friday. The overcast skies of the day before were clearing and there was full sunshine by lunch period. Shadow Point Park would be drying out.

Keesha caught up with her at her locker as they gathered their homework books for the weekend. *Do you want to come over after practice today?*

I'm not going to practice. Library research.

Keesha's brown eyes narrowed. *More research?*

Sara hesitated. *I'll see you tonight. Let's hang out after dinner. Then I'll explain.*

Explain what? You're not up to something without me, are you?

She shook her head and shooed her friend off toward Liz who was standing outside the locker-room door. What Keesha didn't know she couldn't be accused of hiding. Sara felt guilty enough about her own lies, but she drew the line at involving her friend in more than what was absolutely necessary. A

twinge made her frown as she watched Keesha greet Liz.

Downtown in the main detectives' bureau
men and women were assigned to unravel the
mystery of the bridge collapse and Patrick
Martinson's role in it. She knew from her father that they'd start with the crime and work
their way backwards until the pieces fit together. At the fourth precinct Steve Howell
was trying to fit pieces of his father's death
into the same puzzle. She could barely stand
to think that the two might connect.

Sara left the campus by the usual route, but
not before she spotted Lt. Marino again. The
undercover detective was in jeans and a
striped shirt. She blended in with dozens of
parents arriving for a soccer game. Sara gave
no indication that she'd seen her.

The green sedan was in the underground
parking garage at Thurston Court, but Sara
didn't dare take it in case her brother came
home and found it missing. By bike it would
take half an hour to get to the park.

Sara walked home, and entered her building through the parking garage to avoid John

O'Connor. The doorman wouldn't think a thing of mentioning her arrival to Steve. She changed into running shoes and biking shorts, and put away both her school clothes and her backpack. Tuck was up and anxious for attention, but Sara only ruffled his fur and promised a long walk later. "Later," she said. "Good dog."

She grabbed her father's binoculars and her biking gloves and helmet and left as quietly as she'd arrived, by the service elevator off the kitchen entrance. Unlike the pristine front lobby and elevator, the service route always smelled exotic, of hot gourmet meals from a fashionable caterer, or fresh upholstery from someone's new furniture, even fabric softener or flowers. Today she inhaled stale cigarettes again, an odor that lingered well into the underground area. She searched the space while she unlocked her mountain bike and left the minute the lock was unfastened.

She reached Harrison Street at a comfortable speed, but had to stop abruptly to push the hair away from her eyes. As she gripped her handbrakes, and balanced at the curb, two cars passed. She glanced at the third. It was the black sedan without the vanity plate. Sara's adrenaline surged as she watched the rear lights come on. The driver was tapping the brake. Because I stopped, she thought with sickening clarity. She was being followed.

*** *** **** *** *** *** *** ***
*** *** *** *** *** *** ***
*** *** *** *** *** *** *** ***
*** *** *** *** *** *** *** ***
*** *** *** *** *** *** *** ***
***

Chapter 14

It had never been Kimberly Roth. Sara mounted her bike and took the first right down a rutted alley past refuse bins and parked cars. She swerved to miss a group of kids on in-line skates, then jammed her hand-brakes as she reached the street. The black sedan had turned right, as well, and was inching its way through a green light at the corner. Rather than hold up traffic, it continued straight ahead along the boulevard, the same route she had driven yesterday afternoon to the park.

Sara backtracked. Instead of entering Shadow Point Park from the main entrance, she pumped her way back up the hilly east end of Radley toward the cemetery. Outside the gates the sun shone; dogs ran with their owners and two mothers pushed strollers along the sidewalk. It was nearly four o'-clock. They were thinking about dinner, babies' naps, and what movie to rent for the evening. Normal people with normal lives, she thought as she sped through the entrance.

The first wave of anxiety washed over her as she approached her parents' plot. She kept up speed and pumped the pedals as if the sedan were on her heels, as if she could beat her fear. She hit the far side of the cemetery before adrenaline reached her head or her heart or whatever it was that made her feel like she was careening. Riverside Cemetery; nothing but headstones and the place her mother had been for far too long, the place neither of her parents should be.

When she was convinced that she'd lost the car, she biked into the undergrowth, through the trees, and didn't stop until she was in the woods. The trail was still damp. Clots of dirt caught in her tires and flew like handfuls of chocolate cake. Sara squeezed the brakes and slowed herself, well before bursting out into the sunshine at the top of the Shadow Point Trail. At the place where she'd stopped with Liz and Keesha, she locked her bike and bent over nearly double to try and slow her heart.

Followed. Trailed. Someone wanted to know where she was going. Someone knew where she had been. She panted in short shallow breaths, then grabbed the binoculars and set off for the closed trail and the bridge base. This time she went by way of the trees and the undergrowth. A twig scratched her arm as she crept along. She prayed she was being quiet, that she hadn't snapped a limb or scattered birds.

The air was clean smelling and the breeze steady. No warnings, no premonitions haunted her, but her hands still shook. She focused the glasses on the undergrowth as if the black sedan might be parked in the bushes and then chided herself for being so ridiculous. For all she knew it might have been Kim who had passed her this time. It might have been anyone. It was an expensive car, but there were certainly more than two in the city of Radley. She looked up under the bridge, into the mass of girders and forced herself to concentrate. She swept the woods then cautiously moved forward with the binoculars at her eyes.

DANGER WARNING DANGER
TRAIL TO SHADOW POINT CLOSED
DO NOT TRAVEL BEYOND THIS
LOCATION

The capital letters shouted at her and she stepped back. Relax, she ordered herself. Keep a clear head. The Howell motto. She smiled and took her own advice.

When her breathing was steady again, she looked under the bridge. Blue filled the lens; she'd found the tarp. She swung left: a half gallon juice carton sat in the dirt, next to what looked like a stack of newspapers. She panned to the right and found a dark red box with a sneaker logo. There was a large cardboard box and makeshift bedding. Nothing else. The shadows were deep. There was no sign of movement, or life, except for the scattered items. She knew then. Some homeless person was living under the bridge.

Another deep breath. Sara looked up for a

hole in the foliage and watched the patch of blue and a drifting cloud while she slowed her breathing for the hundredth time. She focused the glasses back on the camp. No one.

She counted to one hundred, then two hundred, then she read her watch. After ten minutes with no change, Sara came out of the woods. She slipped around the warning sign to the bridge base. Scattered debris still lay where it had fallen on Sunday. She bent down. There was nothing among the scrap that looked like it had fallen accidentally. She was convinced it had been dropped to scare her away.

She forced herself forward. The binoculars banged against her breastbone on the thin strap as she leaned to the bridge footing. She swore when her knuckles scraped the granite. Blood smeared on a block as she worked her way up around the cement footing to the hillside.

Mud splattered up her shins. Her shirt clung to her and by the time she reached the tarp, she was sweating, sticky and streaked with dirt, bits of grass and twigs. In less than ten minutes she was at the camp wedged between the landscaping and the dank safety of the Shadow Point Bridge.

Her anxiety began to meld with excitement and the steady rhythm of the afternoon traffic overhead. The vibrations were constant. Engineers designed these spans to absorb the continual demands of weight and speed. She looked up. Some place up there, where the bridge stretched across the ravine, the girders had snapped, buckled in on themselves. Sara shuddered and tried not to think about it. Instead she looked left, then right, then over to the parking lot.

She imagined that she was homeless, that she had fashioned a camp under a newly repaired bridge, closed off from the public . . . a safe spot away from the world. Safe except that one Saturday afternoon, in an equally obscure part of the parking lot there was an accident. In front of her eyes.

Patrick Martinson. She blinked and wished she could dismiss the thought that his recklessness with the bridge construction might have had something to do with the death of her father.

Sara inspected the tarp. It was new, still

creased with the folds from its packaging. She could smell the plastic; maybe stolen from the marine supply store at the bottom of the hill. It was propped open with bits of metal debris and tree branches. Cigarette butts were piled in an impromptu dirt ashtray. There were still puddles in the folds from the rain, but the inside bedding was dry. The tent worked. She lifted the juice container. Half full. The newspapers, however, were from summer, dated July and August. He or she might have been here for a month. He or she might have answers.

She sat still and thought about the homeless shelters in Radley. As part of his police work Steve knew all of them and many of the transients who stayed for short periods of time. Maybe someone in one of them would know who the person who lived here was. Maybe Steve would know.

While she collected her thoughts she looked out at the view. She could see the closed trail, the distant river, and the parking lot. The back tier where she'd parked yesterday, where her father had parked, was clear if she peered around the bridge footing.

Sara sighed and leaned back. As she sat, she reached, then stopped with her hand poised above the shoe box. She was intruding, no better than a thief. This was someone's house, she reminded herself, someone who might have witnessed a murder. She gingerly opened the lid of the box: a toothbrush; an empty deodorant container; two candy bars, newspaper articles, and a snapshot. She held the photo and slid into the brighter light. It was of two men in their late twenties standing in front of a stand of birch trees. Any men. Any trees. She flipped it over but the back was blank. As she picked up the newspaper pieces, her curiosity was replaced with guilt. She was intruding no matter what her excuse.

Sara knelt and opened the scraps of newspaper: HIT AND RUN KILLS RADLEY DETECTIVE. The second one was dated two days later. STILL NO LEADS IN COP'S DEATH. The power of the words nearly threw her over the edge of the bluff.

For five minutes Sara kept her head between her knees. When she was sure she wouldn't faint, she put the clippings back with the other items. She was dizzy, light-headed with shock. She signed to the wind. *Who are you? Where are you? Did you see it? Do you know something?*

She forced her impatience down with her fear. Whoever this person was, he or she knew something. Maybe nothing more than another crumb in this Hansel and Gretel trail, but maybe something big, something significant. She hugged her knees and stared at the park grounds. A four-wheel-drive vehicle towing a motorboat worked its way from the marina up through the parking lot and out the entrance. A mother strapped her toddler into his carseat and put the stroller in the trunk of her imported sports car. Normal day. Normal routine. She took a deep breath and ached for anything in her life to feel normal.

The longer she sat, the more impatient she became. She was lost in thought, barely focused on the city parks truck that stopped at the trash barrels to check for refuse. As the worker lifted the barrel over his head, another car slid slowly behind and parked. The car.

Sara snapped to attention and put the binoculars to her eyes. The license was obscured by the refuse bin, but she could see the door was open. Jeans, boots, baseball cap. Cigarette in his mouth. Camera around his neck. She wiped one hand, then the other on her pants. Her binoculars shook; she gripped harder. The photographer. He put the camera to his eye and panned the banks of prize-winning rhododendrons, azaleas, laurels, over . . . to her.

Sara wedged back into the shadow and inched her way toward the edge of the tarp. He finished his cigarette. The minute he lowered his head and stubbed the cigarette under his boot, she scrambled for the cover of trees and stumbled back to her bike.

Sara raced home, steeling herself for her brother's anger. She needed Steve. Her one hope was that when he learned what she'd discovered, he'd forgive her for the way she'd discovered it. That thought got her as far as Harrison Street. Once she was in sight of Thurston Court reality set in and she entered the apartment's parking garage with her heart in her throat. She was being followed, sure now that the photographer had been the shadowy figure leaving traces of cigarette smoke in the hall that night, and in the parking garage that afternoon. It was a result of her sneaky, underhanded, deceitful, conniving behavior. Somehow she'd have to explain it all to her brother.

She locked her bike and took the elevator directly to the seventh floor. Even as she slid the key in her apartment lock, she prayed that Steve would be at the station, giving her time to sort out what she knew — and what she'd done. She worked the key and slowly pushed back the door.

Tuck bounded to her across the foyer and she knelt to nuzzle his neck. "I hope you're alone," she mumbled into his fur as motion in the living room caught her eye. Sara turned on her haunches and looked into the knees of Lt. Marino. The liaison officer was in the archway with the Howells' portable phone at her ear.

Chapter 15

"Steve! What's happened to Steve?" Sara had no idea how loud she was. The police officer gave no indication that she'd understood. Sara scrambled to her feet. Lt. Marino said something, but motion — commotion — drew Sara's attention. She turned, expecting her brother, but Bret Sanderson was rushing toward her from the coffee table.

What are you doing here? What's happened to Steve? Sara signed.

I stopped on my way home from work to see if they'd found you —

Before any of it had time to register, Sara was pulled into a bone-crushing bear hug. This time it was her brother. Steve held her against his chest with one hand at the back of her head so that she couldn't move. She gasped, or he did, the hug was so tight she couldn't tell. It felt as though he was catching his breath, or cracking her ribs, or both.

As suddenly as she'd been hugged, she was put at arm's length. As if he were afraid to let go of her, Steve held her out in front of him, his wide hands on her shoulders. It was the first time she had a chance to see the fear, relief, and tension in his face.

"What in the name of . . . explanations . . . enough without you jumping in . . . no idea where you were . . . kidnapped."

Say again, Sara signed in confusion when she managed to free herself.

"You'd better start explaining right this minute." Steve tried to sign it, but his attempts at ASL were futile and he balled his fists. "Damn. I don't know the signs for half of this."

"Let me help. I'll sign to Sara. You don't need to stumble around," Bret said. *Watch me. I'll interpret for your brother,* he added in sign. His hands picked up the rhythm of the detective's words as well as his anger. He punched the air. *You're all right? Were you followed? I've been frantic. Lt. Marino reported that you weren't at crew practice. She had to break her cover and ask one of the rowers where you were.*

She was tracking me? Sara signed to Steve as Bret said it in English.

"Yes."

That's why she's been at school? You've had me followed? You don't trust me? I don't understand.

You told your coach you were going to the library. More research for your paper, you said. That's what the rower told Lt. Marino. She left Shelter Island and went over to make sure. She found Bret who said you weren't there and hadn't been all afternoon. Bret sighed and stopped Steve long enough to add, *That put me in a panic, too, Sara.* His wide brown eyes grew serious as he resumed interpreting for her brother.

When you weren't at the city library, Rosemary thought she'd misunderstood and went back to the school library.

Guilt drove the dreaded flush up from Sara's collar. She stayed quiet.

No one at either library had seen you. She

called me in and I tracked Bret down again at the Penn Street branch where you told me you'd been on Wednesday. The fact that you weren't there was terrifying enough, but when Bret told me what you'd been researching two days ago — the bridge collapse . . .

Bret shrugged to Sara in apology, but never missed a cue.

What on earth made you decide to play detective? We got back here and found your bike missing . . . You finally show up, you're in biking clothes . . . grubby . . . God, is that blood? Steve examined her hands and caught his breath. Bret flexed his knuckles.

"It's nothing," she said.

Lt. Marino interrupted by hugging her and adding that she was due back at the station. "You gave me a scare, Sara. As long as you're here and safe, I'll leave the rest to your brother."

Steve nodded and waved her off.

Her brother's expression stayed grim as he spoke again and Bret signed. *You don't know how much I'd love to believe that you just played hookey this afternoon.*

I went biking in the park. That much was true.

"Biking in the park!" Steve recoiled as if he'd been slapped. The flush of anger paled to a deadly white, and Lt. Marino turned from where she'd stood by the door. She shook her head as if warning Steve.

Sara looked from Lt. Marino to her brother, aware that neither would dissect her behavior in terms of a police case in front of an innocent teenager. Bret was signing fluently, but his expression had changed to a combination of bewilderment and curiosity.

The only way out of this was to reverse the conversation. Sara tried to look indignant and kept her mouth clamped shut as she signed back to Bret. *Tell my brother I'm sixteen years old. He can't waste taxpayers' money by putting a police tab on me!*

Steve knit his eyebrows. *Say again.*

"Sara says she's sixteen and you're wasting taxpayers' money by having her followed."

She fought the awful heat of another flush as she realized how childish she must appear to Bret by refusing to speak when she signed to Steve. She circled her heart to both of them and spoke as she raised her hands. *"I'm sorry I worried you. I did go biking in the park. I've gone there for years — "* She glanced at Bret, warmed by his still-concerned expression. Could she trust him with what she'd discovered? She sighed. Trust wasn't the issue. The rest of her confession had to be private. Everything she knew or suspected had to be confidential.

Bret seemed to realize what she was thinking. He tapped his watch. *"I need to get home unless you still need me to interpret."*

Steve shook his head as the color returned to his face. "Thanks for your help, all of it. Sara and I can take care of the rest."

Sara walked Bret to the front door. *Thanks. I'm sorry you got dragged into this. I really can take care of myself just fine. Steve and I communicate okay when he's not in a total rage.*

Go easy on him, Bret signed. *I know you can't tell me what's going on, but I can tell that it's serious. I'm glad I could help you,*

Sara, but I want you safe, too. My heart nearly ripped through my chest when Lt. Marino took me aside at the reference desk and flipped her badge open, then asked about you. He paused awkwardly. *I care what happens to you, too. Be careful.*

Thanks. I will be. Maybe when it's all over, I can explain everything to you.

I'd like that. He grinned. *I'll see you Saturday. Is eleven okay? A river picnic might be too calm and boring for you.*

Calm and boring is exactly what I need.

Good. The boat's at Shadow Point Marina.

Sara groaned inwardly. Nothing about Shadow Point, from the park to the marina, was calm, let alone boring. She managed to smile as he left for the elevator. She turned back to the living room slowly.

Steve was waiting. Like all the Howells he ran on adrenaline and instinct. She knew, even before she looked at his face, that he suspected there had been far more to her afternoon than biking in Shadow Point Park.

"I need to tell you what happened this afternoon," she said as she went into the living room.

Steve was back on the couch, looking at papers in his lap. He didn't respond. Not loud enough, she thought. Sara tapped him. *"I went to the park for a reason and you need to know what I found this afternoon, even if it gets me into more trouble."*

"Is Bret gone?"

She nodded, perplexed by the anguish that had replaced the anger in his expression. Steve's hands were shaking. "You need to know why Lt. Marino's been tailing you all week. *Understand?*" He cupped her chin.

She nodded.

Slowly Steve put one arm around her shoulder. Instead of comfort, it filled her with dread. With the other he handed her a photograph. It was black and white, developed on flimsy paper. It was of her. She was in her crew jacket in front of the town houses on her way to school. Monday morning, she thought as she glanced at the computer printed message pasted to the bottom: LEAVE THE BRIDGE ALONE, ROOKIE. YOU'VE GOT ENOUGH TO WORRY ABOUT.

Her throat tightened as her vocal cords vibrated. Had she cried out? Steve tightened his grip and held her up. With his free hand he pulled a second photo off the coffee table. This time two photos were glued back to back. One side showed her rowing. The other side had been taken at the park, shot with a telephoto lens. She stood in the parking lot, hand shading her eyes, looking up at the bridge. Pain shot through her as she skimmed the second note. ROOKIE, HAVEN'T YOU BURIED ENOUGH HOWELLS IN RIVER-SIDE CEMETERY?

Chapter 16

"You never said anything," Sara said.

"There was no point in scaring you. *No point. I didn't want to frighten you, but maybe I was wrong. Maybe fright would keep you where you belong.*"

She pointed to the first note. "You said you weren't working on the bridge case."

"*I'm not. It's Dad's —* " He stumbled for the signs and shrugged.

"*F-I-L-E.*" She finger spelled.

Steve touched his forehead with his fist and raised his index finger, the sign for *Understand.*

Sara took a deep breath. "Now we both know the two cases overlap. *Dad suspected something about the bridge and you think he was killed for what he knew."* She swallowed. *"I'm right, aren't I?"*

At first Steve didn't answer. Then he finally made a fist and thrust it forward. *Yes.* He covered his face with his hands.

Murder. Paul Howell's death might have been murder. The fact had floated so long at the back of her mind, she had no reaction. What good would more grief, more tears, more anger do? Steve straightened up and Sara ran her fist and index finger of her right hand against the open palm of her left to show him the sign. *Murder.* Steve repeated it, then shoved his fists in his pockets and charged from the room.

She found him in the kitchen at the sink. He cupped water in his hands and splashed it on his face, then ran his hands through his hair. "The photos don't make sense," she said with her hand on his shoulder.

He turned to face her. "Sara! Extortion and threats on lives are made by desperate people. Someone wants me to know what you've been up to and to keep us the hell away from the bridge."

"That's what I mean. I know who the photographer is, at least I can identify him. He's still around. He followed me this afternoon at the park."

Say again.

"*I saw the guy take my picture, on the street. It bugged me. Rude. I thought he was part of the same press guys who hounded us when Dad died. That afternoon he was shooting again on the island during crew practice — me, Liz. He wasn't hiding. He had on a* Gazette *jacket. Understand?*"

Steve threw up his hands in defeat. "You could identify him?"

"*Sure. Remember Tuesday when I was looking at the* Gazette *in your office? I was trying to see if his shots made the sports section. They didn't. I should have mentioned it.*"

"You were too busy trying to look innocent. This afternoon when I was trying to figure out what you were up to, I realized why you'd been in my office. You didn't come to apologize; you rifled Dad's file. I should have you locked up. Maybe I still will. It'll keep you out of harm's way." *Keep you safe.*

You need to know about this afternoon. Then you can get angry all at once.

He leaned back against the counter. "You're not dead or kidnapped. I guess anything's better than that. Go ahead." *Tell me everything.*

"I was on my bike. That's the truth. I went back to the park." Her brother cringed but she kept going, slowly, methodically speaking and signing so he'd get every word. *"Think back to the afternoon Dad was killed. Did you know anything was wrong with the boat?"*

"No."

"When you asked to help, Dad said you weren't needed. Then he made us go to the festival together. Why did he park so far away from the marina, way back next to the bridge footing? Why did he send us to something to occupy the same amount of time he needed at Shadow Point?"

"Sara, the department's been over this — "

"He might have been going to look at the bridge, but that doesn't seem logical because it was getting dark. Maybe he was meeting somebody there, somebody who killed him, or had him killed and made it look like an accident. It would have stayed an accident ex-

cept maybe there was a witness and that witness is camped under the bridge, back in the landscaping. The trail's been closed for more than a year. It's safe. From this guy's camp, from the ledge of the footing, the view to where Dad's car was is clear. Perfect. I've checked. I drove the car out there yesterday before I went grocery shopping. I parked in the same spot."

"While Lt. Marino thought you were in the van with the rest of the team, and meanwhile that same guy followed you out there."

She nodded painfully. *"Remember — when I told you about the wind at the park on Sunday, like I was getting a message?"*

Steve shot both open hands into the air, as if he were stopping traffic. *Hold it right there. This isn't some kid's mystery —* He pounded his fist on the counter. "Damn, I wish I knew the signs. If your buddy Bret were a cop I could tell him everything and he could interpret — " He took a deep breath. "This won't be solved by some harebrained snooping teenager."

He took a deep breath as if he were forcing himself to slow down. "You can't run around playing detective. You found some poor homeless guy's camp. Okay. Playing cop doesn't mean you're thinking like one." He poked his temple. "I've been out there with our car, too. Radley's whole detective division's been out there since the accident. Even undercover once things settled down. No one found a camp, Sara. There was nothing there when Dad was killed."

"Maybe he was there when Dad got killed and left till he thought it was safe to come back."

Steve raked his hair again. "Your life's been threatened and I don't know if it's because of the investigation of Martinson Engineering or the snooping around after nonexistent clues about Dad. It doesn't matter. I'll quit the force before I put you at risk."

"Not over me! We've both wanted to be cops since we were kids. It's your dream." She smiled ruefully. *"Dad always said you can't let the bad guys beat you. Lock me in the apartment if you have to."*

Steve looked at her for a long, silent moment. "I want you to think about going back to Edgewood. Somebody's using you to get to me. Putting you back in Edgewood might be the best thing." He turned to the sink and she lost his words.

Say again.

"Somebody's following you to scare me off. Well, it worked. Your old boarding school is the best place for you."

How recently had she ached for the tranquility and security of the school and her friends and the deaf community. She shook her head and fought tears, but they squeezed out through her lashes. *"I'd be sick with worry. I wouldn't be able to study. You're all I have, Steve. Don't send me away."*

He stared at the ceiling, then back at her. "You're all I have, too. That's why I want you there."

"Not yet. Let's see how things go." While he was pensive instead of angry, she decided to finish the confession. *"You need to know about this afternoon. Promise you won't interrupt. Promise!"*

"Why do I get the feeling you're about to tell me you risked your neck on some wild-goose chase?"

"No wild-goose chase. I went up into the camp when I was sure it was deserted."

Steve's eyes widened, but he stayed quiet and simply nodded.

"Not much there. Bed, tarp. But I found a box. There's a snapshot in it of two guys, maybe a little older than you."

"Sara! You're scaring the wits out of me. Promise you won't — "

"Steve, in the box with the picture there's also Gazette *clippings about the accident, about Dad. The person up there knows something. And there's juice. Maybe the person wasn't there before, but whoever it is is there now."*

"And the photographer who's tailing you and threatening us knows it, too."

She began to shiver. *Yes. He followed me again. I know the car. I saw the driver. He smokes. I think I saw — and smelled — him here, too, in the building.*

Chapter 17

Sara barely slept. The realization that Patrick Martinson might have had something to do with the death of her father played in her head like a recurring nightmare. She tried to blot it out by concentrating on other aspects of the unsolved mystery, but she was well down the Hansel and Gretel trail and every crumb and clue turned into fitful images and skewed dreams as she tried to sleep. How could she look Liz in the eye? She thought again of the haven of Edgewood.

"How long am I grounded?" Sara asked the following morning.

Once Steve had listened to her story, he'd

sent the police department to follow up and investigate the campsite. He'd told her at breakfast that even though the officers had arrived after dark, the site had obviously been vacated. It was deserted, with the exception of empty paper cups and a half empty juice container. Sara figured it was one of the reasons Steve had agreed that she could keep the date that afternoon. She could pretend life was normal — even when she glanced up under the bridge girders.

Grounded? The rest of your life. Steve dropped his hands as he answered. "You're damn lucky I'm letting you keep your date with Bret. For that matter you're lucky Keesha's not in the Penn Street lockup as an accomplice for all your illegal activities."

"I might have been sneaky, but nothing was illegal. Keesha hardly did anything." *Anything.*

"No arguing. You're grounded for the weekend. I want you safe."

She stared back at Steve, secretly relieved that she wouldn't have to face Liz until school on Monday.

"Enjoy the afternoon while you're out on parole," he was saying. *Enjoy. Just remember —*

"I know, I know." She held up her fingers and counted in sign. *One: Go on the boat only. No park, no trail. Two: Directly home. Three: —* She paused and added her voice. *"If I see Lt. Marino I should pretend I don't know her."* Steve flushed and she pointed to his cheeks. "I knew it. You're going to have me followed."

"Threats, Sara. You either go with an escort or stay home."

"Or go back to Edgewood," she added.

Don't. It's for your safety, you know that. He touched her arm. "It won't be Rosemary. Bret's not to know and he would recognize her. More likely Hank Allen from downtown."

She scrunched her fingers in front of her face.

"Don't get angry; get used to it." He shrugged. "Who knows, when boys take you for picnics I may always have somebody in the bushes with binoculars."

Sara swatted at him. *Not funny.* It wasn't

funny. Threats on her life were terrifying, and although she'd never admit it, having a cop somewhere within shouting distance was a comforting thought. For the first date, anyway.

The banter killed the butterflies in her stomach, but the thin lines at her brother's eyes and his pursed mouth told her he was as determined as she was to make her routine normal.

Unlike the rainy week and the deserted park of Thursday and Friday, Shadow Point Marina was bustling. The September Saturday was balmy and the intermittent clouds posed no threat. She and Bret were dressed alike in jeans and T-shirts, and she'd pulled her long brown hair into a ponytail. From the moment they took the apartment elevator he was relaxed and funny. She tried valiantly to match his mood. He signed fluently and it gave her an excuse to watch his handsome, animated face without blushing.

They parked in the middle of the parking lot. As Bret closed his car door, Sara unconsciously squinted up at the furthest brace of the bridge and the now empty hillside under it. It filled her with foreboding. Bret put his hand on her shoulder and she jumped. *Are you okay?*

She nodded.

Want to tell me about it?

No! I want to get in the boat and put the wind on my face and forget everything connected with the stupid bridge. She tried to smile at him, make it into a joke, but her expression faded into a long pensive glance as his eyes read hers. She was grateful that he was perceptive enough not to tell her what he saw. Instead he hoisted the picnic basket between them and led her to the slip that held the Sanderson twenty-three-foot day cruiser.

She scanned the parking lot for any sign of a cop she might recognize. Bret Sanderson would be out of her life like a rocket if she told him they were being followed.

They spent the afternoon skimming the shoreline, cruising the open waterway around the bend, at the base of the Tenth Street bridge that led to Shelter Island. They moored the boat in the shallows and picnicked in a clearing where someone had laid a campfire. From the shore of the island Sara watched tugboats push coal barges, and pleasure boats cruise. Behind them, rowers glided along the narrow channel between the island and the shore.

Bret never broached the subject of the bridge or her mood. Instead, he signed about rowing, school, his little brothers, and how good Penham's basketball team was going to be.

She relaxed, even laughed and when he kissed her, she wondered again which detective had the two of them in his binoculars and how much would get reported back to her brother. At four o'clock they returned to the marina and moored the boat back in its slip. She pointed out the Howell powerboat and promised next time they'd use hers.

Bret pressed his index finger against the tight frown lines between her eyebrows. *I got them to disappear for the first time since you came into the library. You need to do this more often.*

Boats?

He grinned and pressed his forehead against hers before signing: *Boats with me in them.*

Sara laughed and thought about how good it felt.

On the way to the parking lot Bret snapped his fingers and stopped. *I need a couple of minutes in the marine supply shop. Cleat for the foredeck.*

While he shopped in the marine supply section, Sara perused the boutique area, looking at boat shoes, high style T-shirts and rowing paraphernalia. When she caught up with Bret he was at the counter with his back to her paying for the hardware.

While he folded the receipt and put it in his wallet, she glanced at the Plexiglas countertop. Underneath were years' worth of postcards, business cards, and photographs customers had added to and enjoyed. Throughout her childhood her father had waited while she skimmed the postcards and guessed at the locations. The memory tugged as she glanced at the latest arrivals.

All set? Bret signed.

She nodded. *My dad used to bring me in*

here and point out all the exotic locations in the postcards and pictures. She smiled and quickly looked them over. She would have started for the door if her glance hadn't landed on a snapshot that riveted her to the floor. Unconsciously she grabbed Bret's arm as the shock of what she was seeing registered in the pit of her stomach. A color photograph was wedged between a view of Niagara Falls and a card from Paris. It was a five-by-seven-inch version of the snapshot in the shoebox under the bridge. Birch trees. Two men in their twenties side-by-side. Identical to the one she'd found in the camp. She bit her lip and tried desperately not to look shocked.

You okay?

She nodded numbly, aware that he didn't believe her for a moment. When she was sure of the strength in her knees, she started for the door, Bret beside her.

Once they were out in the daylight, he signed again. *I'm sorry it was such a shock seeing the picture of B-R-I-A-N. Did you know him very well?*

Who? Sara asked.

Bret frowned in confusion. *B-R-I-A-N S-T-R-E-E-T*, he finger spelled. *In the photo. The guy on the right was killed in the bridge collapse. He worked here at the marina. I thought you must have known him and that's what upset you, with your father's death being fresh in your mind and everything.*

Tears sprang to her eyes and cupped in her lashes, tears from fatigue and fear and confusion and the awful need to sink onto the curb and try to make sense of what kept falling into her lap. Whoever was camped under the bridge might have seen a murder and kept a photograph of one of the victims in the bridge collapse. She wanted to explain, to open her heart. She didn't. She couldn't, but when Bret hugged her, she took a deep breath and stayed still, leaning against his chest, feeling the steady rhythm of his heart.

Chapter 18

"**Y**ou're sure you didn't explain anything?"

Across their kitchen table, Sara gave her brother her most disgusted look. *Explain? I made B-R-E-T bring me home so fast he probably thinks it was the worst date of my life. Some date. I get kissed with cops watching then find a major clue to a murder and I can't tell my date anything.* She pointed at Steve. "You do the explaining. All I know is that whoever is under the bridge has the same picture and a connection to the two guys in it. One's dead. Do you understand?" She began to shiver.

Steve Howell finger spelled without speaking. *Okay, B-R-E-T told you B-R-I-A-N S-T-R-E-E-T worked for the marina and was*

*killed in the bridge collapse. His brother is
A-D-A-M* — Steve tapped his lip to indicate
that she was to pay close attention as she lip-
read. "I've been looking for him, for Adam
Street. Are you sure it's the same photo as the
one you found?"

She nodded. "Smaller. Yes." She closed
her fingers and sliced both hands forward to
sign: *Street. You weren't looking for a street
in Radley, you were looking for someone with
the* name *Adam Street?*

It was plain Steve was trying to decide
how much to reveal. *I wrote it on the mirror,
remember?* he signed.

She nodded and watched her brother sink
deep into thought. He got up from the table
slowly, almost painfully, and grabbed his car
keys from the hook by the door.

Twenty minutes later he'd maneuvered
their sedan across the city to the arched stone
entrance to Riverside Cemetery. He finally
pulled the car over when they'd wound their
way down along the hedges that separated
the burial plots from the woods. As he took
the keys from the ignition, Sara reached for

the door handle, but he grabbed her hand and tapped his mouth.

"Don't leave my side. Just as I said before we left, if I get officers out here from the station, it'll just call more attention to what we need to do. I want you to show me how you went in on Sunday with Keesha and Liz, then how you came up when you were alone this week. Stay next to me and stay quiet. When we're finished I'm turning all the information over to my department and you're not to set foot back here. Got it?"

She nodded, more than happy to agree.

"I've put you at risk enough already."

Sara started off hoping she looked far calmer than she felt. The path she'd taken on Sunday with Liz and Keesha behind her on their mountain bikes opened up from the dense walking trails that rimmed the cemetery. A few families were walking the lanes, but once she lead Steve to the woods, the trail was deserted. This time she saw a small sign, nearly covered by foliage. TRAIL CLOSED AHEAD NO ACCESS TO SHADOW POINT OR MARINA. How different her life would be if she'd seen it last Sunday.

They walked quickly until they reached the tree where she'd propped her bike. She swept her arm to show their path and the bridge looming above them. Steve studied the shadows and the area behind the first footing until she tapped his shoulder.

"What do you know about Adam Street?" Sara asked.

He shrugged.

Steve! *"I'm involved in this whether you like it or not. Right now I don't even like it! Keeping secrets might only put you or me at greater risk."*

He nodded painfully. "Okay. I used to see Brian at the marina. He knew Dad and I were cops and he came to us one time when Adam was missing. Adam Street has problems with depression. He fights mental illness like lots of the homeless. He and his brother had no other family, but Adam lives in an excellent halfway program across the river: Hillsboro House. Dad arranged it. When Brian died in the bridge collapse, Adam started disappearing for a few days at a time. It's hard on him. I found him last winter near the docks. He's usually gone back to Hillsboro House on his own. This time he's been gone since the middle of last month. Missing persons called me to see if I could shake the bushes again."

"The call didn't have anything to do with this case?"

"Not directly." *No. Not this case or the other one.*

"The other one? Come on, Steve, I know the truth as well as you do. Liz's father's mess with the bridge and Dad's mess with the bridge are probably the same case."

"Okay," he added painfully.

"The first time you found him, or the time at the docks — did you ever find Adam Street under a bridge?" *Under a bridge?*

Slowly Steve nodded.

"Maybe he feels safe," *feels safe,* she added with her hands, *"under bridges. Understand? He came here to feel closer to his dead brother, to feel safe. The halfway house said he disappeared the middle of last month. Maybe he came back here for comfort and just happened to be here when Dad was killed. Understand? Understand! Coincidence. He witnessed Dad's murder and has been hiding out ever since."*

Steve's look was so intense Sara finally raised her hands. *What is it?*

You. You'll make a great detective some day, if you don't turn out to be a — He fumbled and shrugged. He tapped his temple and chin: *Head,* then his wrist: *Doctor.*

Sara laughed. "Psychologist. Psychiatrist."

"Yes. Okay, Dr. Detective, show me where you went Sunday."

They turned back to the trail and she pointed and spoke. "Liz and Keesha and I were all here. Liz got upset about the bridge and left. Keesha went after her. When they left I went up closer, around the sign. There was nothing here."

"Can you remember if it looked as though someone might have been here?"

She shook her head. "No campsite, then, but felt like it. Creepy feeling. I got chills, like I was being watched." She made a fist and opened her index and middle finger, pushing them forward. *Watched.* When Steve nodded, she pointed to the debris at the foot of the base. "This wasn't here when I carried my bike under. When I turned around, it was. Maybe somebody yelled and warned me."

She shrugged. "How would I know?" she asked in pain.

Together — close together — they walked around the warning sign and underneath the bridge. She showed him where the campsite had been, and the box she'd opened. Then she turned to scan the parking area. "See? Adam had been up here. He could have seen where Dad's car was parked over next to the footing. He might have seen everything."

"Don't jump to conclusions."

"He has the newspaper clippings. The pieces fit, Steve! Adam Street was here. His brother died in the crash; he's on his own, no other family. Then he witnesses something — and has to hide."

Hide? At the scene of the crime? No sense.

She stopped talking long enough to get a closer look at what had been somebody's home for at least a few days. She waited for the chill and the wind, but there was nothing but the sweet pine smell of the woods and the breeze up off the Buckeye.

Steve made a complete search of the empty space, even climbed the footing. She could almost see the change in him as he let his detective training take over. When he finished, he hadn't turned up anything more than she had. He worked his way down off the cement and moved into the daylight with her. "Gone. You or the photographer probably scared him off."

Sara nodded at the logic. For once something made sense. She'd walked right under Adam Street with her bike on Sunday. Then she appeared again on Thursday in the same car that had been driven by the man he'd seen being killed. Even she had to admit that would be enough to drive anybody away. Logical facts. There hadn't been many.

Steve pointed to the deserted bike trail. "Did you ride over there after you came under the bridge?" *Ride over there?*

Yes. To the parking lot then home through the park entrance. This time there were chills. Right down her back.

They walked along the path. Nothing had changed. The grasses and weeds were still high from lack of use. She was about to turn back when a flat rectangle of bluff caught her eye. Unlike the knee-high grasses blowing in the breeze, the section was darker, flattened.

More construction remnants, she thought, except that it was on a steep pitch of the hill and she hadn't noticed it either of the times she'd combed the hillside looking for signs of who might be under the bridge.

Curious, Sara moved through the grasses until she stumbled as the toe of her sneaker caught on something loose. She yanked her foot back hoping it wasn't a snake, only to find she'd snagged the black neck strap of a camera. She knelt down and picked up the remains of a smashed telephoto lens and empty case. In two bolts she was up on her feet and headed to the high grass. What she found stopped her as quickly as she'd started. The photographer lay sprawled on his back. His open eyes stared, unseeing, at the traffic moving above him on the Shadow Point Bridge.

Steve reached her as she half knelt, half stood, as stiff as the body. Then, as if someone had synchronized their movements, she and her brother both turned to look at the campsite.

Chapter 19

Sara pushed her dinner around on her plate and watched as peas rolled into the mashed potatoes. Steve was on the phone for the third time since they'd sat down. He held the receiver with one hand and clenched and unclenched the other as he talked, then hung up.

All he would tell her was that the body had been identified as George Resnik, a minor thug with no known photojournalistic connections to the *Gazette* or any other paper. His criminal record was for petty theft, and two recent traffic violations had been added for double-parking in front of the courthouse.

Steve admitted that wearing a *Gazette*

jacket and carrying forged press credentials might serve as a cover. Nobody would suspect anything as he shot photos of a teenager in a rowing jacket and action shots of a popular sport.

Even the teenager wouldn't suspect, Sara had added. Athletes were easy subjects and published regularly in the neighborhood section of the paper.

"Nevertheless," Steve replied, "this freelance job was probably done for someone else, someone who hired him to track you long enough to scare me off the case."

"Someone who worked in the courthouse where he double-parked and ran in with the developed photos?" Sara guessed.

Her brother narrowed his gaze. "You're too perceptive for your own good."

Say again.

P-E-R-C-E-P-T-I-V-E.

She shrugged. *I'll make a good cop.*

"You're not one, yet, so knock it off."

The phone rang again. She tried to read his lips as he talked, but he turned his head — purposely, she suspected. He turned back and took a sip from his glass. She read: "Nothing? Not even in the soup kitchen on Market Street? Okay. Keep trying." Steve pivoted as Tuck trotted to him. He leaned and ruffled his fur. "Yes . . . keep me posted," was all Sara could get as she took a half-hearted bite of the potatoes.

Her brother sat back down. "Cause of death was a broken neck, maybe sustained in a fall from the underpinnings of the bridge."

Or maybe from being pushed off by Adam Street? You're thinking he's a suspect. Aren't you?

"Never mind what I'm thinking. And don't you do any thinking. Nothing makes sense yet."

But it will. A criminal who doesn't take many precautions to disguise himself must have thought he wasn't involved in anything too risky or serious. Maybe someone lied to him about the assignment. Someone set him up, someone really dangerous who maybe meant to get rid of him all along, once the pictures were taken.

Steve shrugged. *"Don't get melodramatic. Murder is a messy business."*

Sara ran fist and pointed finger past her open palm. *Murder.*

Steve grimaced and repeated the sign. "Murder is rarely planned, or premeditated. Acts of passion or even accidents like Dad's . . ."

"Maybe weren't supposed to happen?"

Sara, I just don't know.

"This George Resnik was in the wrong place at the wrong time. So was poor Adam."

Steve smiled at her. *Enough junior detective.* "Whatever we learn, we learn officially. Even I have to wait for information from the department since I'm off the case."

Because of me.

"That's the way I want it."

Sara survived the weekend. Keesha knew she'd been grounded, and guessed it had something to do with their detective work, but for her own safety, Steve said only that he'd discovered Sara's skipping crew practice and her trip to the library. Bret called on the TTY and Sara assured him she was fine, even though she was restricted. She didn't mention the photo at the marine store, or her reaction to it, and Bret didn't bring it up, either. She'd acted so squirrelly he was probably afraid to bring up anything. As she typed out their conversation, she wondered what he must be thinking of her. Someday when the puzzle was solved and all the pieces were in place, when the case was long over and settled, she would tell him everything, including where he fit. For now she had to live with the frustration and anxiety of unanswered questions and long-held secrets.

Monday morning the discovery of the dead photographer made the television news. Sara and Steve watched over breakfast, grateful that the news anchor knew only that the body had been discovered by a hiker who'd followed the wrong trail at Shadow Point Park. The police department refused all other comment. Of course it was reported from the park. Crime scene tape now stretched over the top of the trail. If Adam Street had ever thought of returning, he wouldn't now.

One more reason to keep that trail closed,

Steve added as he turned off the set and insisted on driving Sara to school. It was either that or have her under surveillance from the department, he said when she put up an argument.

How long do I have to have my big brother deliver me to the front door?

I don't like it, either. Don't complain or I'll take you in a squad car with the sirens screaming.

She poked her ears. *Can't hear sirens. That would only embarrass you.*

When they reached the curb in front of the school, Steve leaned back and took one long look through the windshield. "Go to class. Go to crew practice. Go home with Keesha. No monkey business."

"You, either." She tapped his chest. *Be careful. No secrets. My whole family — you.*

Steve crossed his heart. *See you at dinner. I'll be home, too, by then.*

After assuring him one more time that she'd be fine, she left him at the curb and walked through Radley Academy's crowded halls. She wasn't worried about herself; she was worried about Steve, only partly relieved that he was going directly to the station. Or so he'd said.

As she approached her locker she paused. Keesha and Liz were waiting for her. Dread threaded through her as she looked at Liz. The girl was smiling innocently and the glance settled in the pit of Sara's stomach. More than anything she wanted to believe that their lives were connected by nothing but friendship, and not the growing suspicion that Patrick Martinson had needed Lt. Paul Howell out of the way once the officer started to investigate the bridge collapse. For the first time in days Sara thought about Steve's plan for the thirtieth. Hidden Acres was beginning to have more appeal than the riverboat party.

As she reached the girls, Sara put on her brightest smile and searched for a safe subject to discuss. She pulled her books from her locker and mentioned her picnic with Bret.

"Were you at Shadow Point Marina on Saturday afternoon?" Liz asked.

Yes. Grounded the rest of the time. B-R-E-T took me out in his —

Dead body.

Sara dropped her hands and slammed her locker shut.

Liz tapped her shoulder. "Did you see the news? Did you know they found George Resnik up at the bridge, right where we were on our bikes last weekend? My father nearly paced a hole in the rug when he found out. He got totally unnerved."

Say again.

"Dead person. Dad went totally ballistic when I told him you'd taken me to the bridge, practically to the same spot. Now the guy winds up dead right where we were. George Resnik. The guy used to work for my father."

Chapter 20

By the time Sara reached the edge of the soccer field, she'd decided that she probably wouldn't be expelled for skipping school. Sure as rowers used oars, she faced suspension, however. She looked back at the school building, then darted across the boulevard, dodging traffic mid-block. Radley Academy's punishment for leaving campus without permission was the furthest thing from her mind.

She'd left Keesha and Liz outside the biology room. She'd left her backpack at the foot of her locker and signed to her interpreter Mrs. Andrews that she had to go home. She was running by the time she crossed the main corridor and once she knew no one was going to stop her, she shoved the fire door open with both hands. If anyone had called after her, she'd never know.

She raced past the townhouses where she'd first seen George Resnik. Fool. Stupid fool. Another knot of commuters waited at the corner for their approaching bus. The crossing guard at Fifth and Lovell avenues was herding a group of kids into the elementary school. Sara stopped to catch her breath and put her hand into the crick in her side. She started up again at a trot in the direction of Penn Street.

The air at Penn and Harrison was thick with the aroma of chocolate. A waiter from the deli was sweeping the sidewalk. She grimaced at the normalcy of a Monday morning in Radley, shoved her hand into her hair to pull it off her face and yanked open the doors of the police station.

The desk sergeant had the phone to his ear and without asking she sprinted past him and took the stairs two at a time. Steve's cluttered office was empty. She moaned, breathless and gulping. Interrogation room. Maybe he was still in one of his roundtable brainstorming sessions. She jogged down the hall, relieved to see that the door was open. Half a dozen officers were gathered at the table in the middle of the narrow space. Rosemary Marino had a cup of coffee. Two officers were in street clothes with shoulder holsters under their arms. One was her brother. Steve was sitting on the edge of the table holding a clipboard which he nearly dropped as she moved into view and motioned for him to come out in the hall.

The minute he joined her, she signed, *Steve. Dead body worked for bridge man.* She repeated her shorthand knowing her brother would never be able to decipher her finger spelling of the proper names, then pressed back again the wall, finally catching her breath.

"What the hell? Sara, are you all right? Did you skip school? How'd you get here?" Steve shook his head, astonished.

She pointed to her feet. *Am I interrupting?*

He took her by the arm — just short of yanking — and walked her back into his office. "What in the name of heaven made you

race over here? You left school! Did you sign
out? Did you tell Mrs. Fletcher?"

"Don't be mad. I had to see you. You have
to know — " A tear escaped from her eye and
she rubbed her cuff over it angrily. Her
brother's grip on her arm loosened and she
let him ease her into his chair. After another
fitful start, she explained the conversation
with Liz. *I had to come. You may be in more
danger. Liz's dad will know who found dead
body — R-E-S-N-I-K. He'll find out it was
you. He knows I took Liz there last week. Understand? He hired dead body to follow me.
He knows from the photos in the parking lot
that I went back, that we all suspect something.*

"Sara, slow down. I'm only getting half of
what you're trying to tell me."

She nodded. "George Resnik worked for
Patrick Martinson." Her fingers flew again.
*Liz's father builds a sloppy bridge. It col-
lapses. Now to keep you off the case, they go
after me. M-A-R-T-I-N-S-O-N sends R-E-S-
N-I-K to follow me and take pictures to scare
you. Some are of me at the bridge. Liz tells*

*her dad I took her there on my bike. Now he
knows for sure that we connect Dad with the
case.* She swiped again as the tears blurred
her vision. "Liz is practically my only friend
in Radley and her own father —" She
couldn't finish. She rubbed her fists against
her eyes and straightened up. "No more tears.
I've cried enough over all of this." *Enough
tears.*

*Tears are good, sometimes. Don't be brave
for me, Sara.* He closed the door and rolled
his partner's chair over, then sat in front of
her. His smile surprised her. He cocked his
head toward the room down the hall. "That
meeting you just blasted into —"

She circled her heart.

"Don't be sorry. No harm done. It was to
tell me that the state attorney's office has in-
dicted a suspect in the case."

Her palms grew clammy.

"It's not Patrick Martinson." *Understand?*
"You have to read my lips. I don't know the
signs for this. Complicated. They're indict-
ing Howard Gillespie." He wrote the name
on a scratch pad.

"They worked together! It was in the newspaper article I read at the library."

Steve nodded. "Gillespie worked for Martinson Engineering and was responsible for the infrastructure of the bridge. Patrick Martinson contracted for top of the line materials, of course, had them inspected and everything. Gillespie sold and replaced the steel for an inferior grade, then kept the money. Never thought anyone would know . . . or that the bridge would collapse. Martinson didn't know. Nobody knew until the district attorney's office looked at Gillespie's orders. They found the motive: huge gambling debts. Martinson trusted him. Didn't know what he was doing. *Understand?"*

Sara nodded.

"Martinson helped the DA put the pieces together, and discovered that Gillespie switched the goods, as we say." *Switched the goods.* Steve grinned when she nodded. "He's been the suspect all along and now he's under arrest."

"But George Resnik."

"Resnik worked for Martinson a few years ago and was arrested for petty theft. That came up on his rap sheet. Once the investigation of Martinson started, Gillespie panicked. He found Resnik and paid him to take those pictures to scare me off the case. He's nearly suicidal over getting caught. He swears switching the steel and sending the photos were all he did. I doubt Resnik fell to his death, but Gillespie swears he had nothing to do with it or Dad's. I believe him."

Sara searched her brother's face before she asked the final question. *"Then who killed Dad?"*

Steve's shrug was slow. *If it's the last thing I ever do, Sara. I'll find out.*

Twenty minutes later Sara was still concentrating on the relief sweeping through her. She smiled at Steve. *Liz's dad's been cleared of doing anything wrong. He isn't a murderer. They know who's responsible for the bridge collapse and he's in jail. Nobody's following me anymore. I guess this means I can go to the riverboat party.*

Steve stood up and tugged her to her feet. *I*

guess this means I can drive you back to school.

The evening of September thirtieth was clear and warm. The relief Sara had felt in her brother's office had stayed with her, dulled only by the frustration that as the month drew to a close, Howard Gillespie still insisted he knew nothing about the deaths of George Resnik or Lt. Paul Howell.

Sara dressed for the Martinson party in her favorite dressy beige linen pants and pink silk shirt, not quite as formal as the adults who would fill the decks of the *Buckeye Queen*. Her hair hung loose in a matching headband, the way Bret liked it. Shortly before six she did a pirouette for Steve in their living room. He gave her a thumbs-up gesture.

Sara made him spin around, as well. Her brother managed to look handsome despite his shaggy hair and four-day growth of beard. Steve's search for Adam Street continued in the homeless shelters, bridges, and soup kitchens on both sides of the Buckeye River. He was dressed for the back streets of

Radley again, this time in a black cotton turtleneck, stained jeans split at the knee, and ripped sneakers.

Sara signed, *Be careful tonight.* "If Adam spots you, he'll know he can trust you, but be careful. Docks at night — "

Always careful. You — don't worry. You — have fun. You — be careful. B-R-E-T — He shrugged and gave up. *Have fun.*

She intended to, but she wished he were off to the movies or dinner with one of the women he dated.

Tuck trotted to Sara to indicate that the doorbell had rung, and she pushed the buzzer to let Bret Sanderson into the downstairs lobby, then opened the apartment door to watch the elevator. When the steel doors parted, she grinned as Bret sauntered down the hall. He smiled. In traditional blazer and tie he looked gorgeous.

He flipped his fingers into, *Hi.*

Hi, yourself, she returned.

Bret came into the apartment, and glanced at the raised newspaper Steve held open in front of him. His grin widened.

Sara poked Bret in the arm. *What did he say?*

Who?

She nodded toward the couch. *You know who! I'm onto that stupid trick. Steve said something to you behind the newspaper. You laughed.* She tapped his mouth.

Color washed Bret's cheeks. *Just advice about getting you home on time. He said if the riverboat doesn't dock by your curfew, we're supposed to jump overboard and swim in.*

Sara swatted the newspaper. *No big brother advice.*

Steve laid it on the coffee table. *Say again.*

"Don't look so innocent." She laughed and continued her protest until a photograph on the back page caught her eye. A middle-aged man in a hard hat, posed in front of scaffolding, was shaking hands with the governor. The caption read: *Thomas Covington retires from Department of Public Works.*

She tapped the paper. "When I spotted Resnik taking my picture from the trail at the boathouse, he was with this guy in the hard hat. They were looking around and I thought he was from the rowing center."

Bret tapped his watch. *"Sorry to interrupt but we have to get Keesha and make the riverboat before it leaves the marina. Jacket? Might be colder on the water."*

Sara didn't like the expression on Steve's face, but there was no time to lose. She opened the foyer closet. Instead of her usual blazer, she pulled on her father's linen sports jacket. Oversized, rolled at the cuffs and a match for her pants, it was fashionable, bittersweet, and oddly comforting.

Be careful of Dad's jacket. Fits me better, Steve signed.

Sara nodded as she pulled folded paper from a pocket. The first was a flyer for the August arts festival's fireworks. The second was a note with her father's familiar handwriting. The burn of grief started in her throat until she read the print:

Saturday
T. Covington
3:15 DPW CC #624

She shoved the papers at Steve. *Dad must have worn this the afternoon he died. Look!*

Steve shook his head, perplexed.

Translate for Steve! she demanded of Bret as her gestures tumbled. She grabbed the newspaper long enough to poke at the photograph again, then signed. *Before Dad left for the marina, he told us about the fireworks, he said he'd been to a meeting at the county courthouse and had seen the festival. Remember! Look! He picked up this flyer. Steve, he met C-O-V-I-N-G-T-O-N. DPW: Department of Public Works. CC — county courthouse. Dad met the same man I saw with R-E-S-N-I-K!*

Bret reluctantly tapped his watch again.

Sara nodded. *"This might be a real lead. Promise tomorrow we can work on it."*

Steve raised his hand, then tapped his chest. "I'll work on it." He patted Bret on the shoulder. "Don't let her stew over this all night and ruin the party."

Sara scowled. *Steve! This could be important.*

I know. I promise. Tomorrow. The only sign that anything was amiss was the set of her brother's jaw and a flash in his blue eyes that faded as she looked into them.

Chapter 21

There was no need to rush. The *Buckeye Queen* was forty-five minutes late leaving the dock, which didn't seem to bother anyone. The guests entered on the gangplank and greeted their hosts in a receiving line that led the party onto the main rear deck. The Martinson family shook hands, hugged, and chatted until the last arrival came aboard.

By the time the boat pulled anchor, and the huge blades of the paddle wheel began to turn, the *Buckeye Queen* was crowded with people. Sara and Bret spotted the mayor and her husband, and members of the city council. Keesha nudged her as they passed the *Gazette*'s columnist for the social pages. The rest, according to Liz, were her parents' life-long friends and business associates. Sara leaned against the rail and admired the designer outfits and evening jackets on the glittering guests.

She was on the main deck across from a dance band that edged the dance floor. Inside a buffet dinner would be laid on the linen-covered tables that already groaned with centerpieces of exotic fruits and flowers that looked to Sara as if they'd been flown in from Hawaii or South America.

Keesha nodded toward a group sampling hors d'oeuvres being passed on a caterer's tray. *How many of these guys would be here if the case hadn't been solved and Liz's dad were still under suspicion?*

True friends, Sara replied with a twinge of guilt. Her own brother hadn't wanted her here. Just days ago she herself had been sure of Patrick Martinson's guilt.

Sara leaned back against the rail and watched the adults mingle. Halfway between herself and the dance floor, two men stood on the separate staircases that led to the upper deck. The first, tall and bald, was halfway up the closest set of stairs; a short, stocky middle-aged man was at the bottom of the second. The flower-wrapped banisters had caught her eye, but it was the men that held her interest. Although they were in tuxedos like the rest of the adults, the cut of their dinner jackets gave them away. Not for nothing was she the daughter and sister of two plain-clothes detectives. Sara Howell could spot the bulge of an underarm holster beneath even the most custom-tailored jacket.

It made sense that the Martinsons would hire security after what they'd been through. She watched the men and wished Steve had been hired to keep an eye on the party. He could look for homeless Adam Street in the daylight.

The riverboat began its leisurely cruise up the wide, meandering Buckeye by gliding beneath the Shadow Point Bridge. After what it had done to his life and reputation, Sara wondered if Patrick Martinson was secretly cringing as they passed under it. She was.

Although it was barely dusk, lights blinked on the trusses, and occasional headlights flashed as cars passed well overhead. They cruised toward the city and Sara purposely stayed on the starboard side of the deck so that her view was of Hillsboro instead of the parking lot that had created such havoc in her own life.

Bret handed her a cheese puff as Liz indicated that they were all invited to move above to their own smaller deck where music and dinner had been planned just for the guests of Liz and her sister Karen.

As the teenagers approached the staircases the armed men stepped down and into the throng of adults. A deejay was in full swing on the deck, taking requests and some of Liz's braver friends were already dancing. The entire class was present, plus a mix of dates like Bret Sanderson who attended other schools. Sara caught sight of Kimberly Roth and wondered if she'd learned that her car was a perfect match for the dead photographer's. It would give her something to discuss if the party got dull.

Sara chose the rail again. From the upper deck she could see the adults, but she also had a spectacular view of the ravines that plunged to the Buckeye River and, well ahead, Radley's glowing skyline. She watched the river churn through the wheel and felt the vibrations of engine and music in the wooden floor.

Keep Steve safe tonight. She signed the wish to the evening star as it began to twinkle at the horizon. There was a tap on her shoulder. She turned to Bret and one glance into his brown eyes told her he had read either her hands or the melancholy expression she knew had changed her features.

He brushed her hair back off her shoulder. *You know why I'm glad you're deaf? The music's so loud I couldn't hear you even if we were speaking. Hands are so easy.* He wiggled his fingers, then put his arms out to her. *Dance with me.*

She shook her head and glanced around. *Some other time. Not in front of hearing kids. They don't know me.*

They don't know me either. He nodded at the couples already in each other's arms. *It's a slow dance. Easy. Follow me, I'm a fabulous dancer.* He pushed his palms out from his forehead, then gestured with his thumb tapping his forefinger. *Wonderful. Perfect,* he signed, then pointed to his feet.

She laughed. Bret Sanderson made her feel wonderful. Perfect.

They danced the next two and if her classmates were watching, it felt like friendly glances and approval. Bret was easy to follow as he tapped out the rhythm on her shoulder. When the music finally stopped, she grinned as she left the dance floor. *Now I'm sorry the music's over. You were right.*

Good, then let's keep dancing. Who needs music?

An hour later on her way to the rest room with Keesha, Sara savored the happiness that had lifted her mood. She cherished her relationship with Bret; she was growing comfortable with her classmates; the moon was up and the stars were out.

And the women's bathroom was full. Keesha held her ears as the two of them waited in the narrow space beneath the stairs. Keesha indicated with a nod that they were directly under one of the amplifiers for the deejay.

The minute a woman came out of the bathroom, Sara insisted Keesha go in. *My ears are fine.*

Thanks. Mine are ringing.

Sara watched the guests as she waited. A man about her brother's age came out of the men's room, followed at separate intervals by the two men she knew were wearing shoulder holsters. Although they gave no indication that they knew each other, they walked side by side and stopped under the amplifier. As the short one began to talk, the bald one kept his glance straight ahead.

"As public as possible . . . No one will ever know who did it." A woman in a sequined cocktail dress came up the stairs. The first man stepped aside to let her pass. When she'd gone, he continued. "A few quick, clean shots, Joe. Take him out while the glasses are raised in that ridiculous toast. Then get yourself overboard."

Sara's heart jumped. Surely she'd misunderstood. A couple worked their way around the men and headed for the bar, but the two kept talking. When they were alone again, the short one dusted his jacket with a sweep of his hand. "After this cruise, I'll pick ⌐ up. I'll be waiting at the east end of Shelter Island."

"See ya, Mac," Joe said. He put his hands in his pockets and left. After a ten-second delay, the second one sauntered off and took the furthest staircase. A third man was coming up. Their eyes met. They nodded and continued in opposite directions.

As the man reached the landing and passed her, Sara turned and frowned as she tried to place him. He went to the rail and leaned against it, looking out at the Hillsboro landscape. As Liz Martinson passed, he shook her hand and patted her on the back. Obviously it was someone friendly with the entire Martinson family. With her heart in her throat and her ears burning, Sara shoved the rest room door back open. *She knew that face.* It was Covington.

Chapter 22

You okay?

Sara blinked into the mirror as she washed her hands and stared at Keesha's curious expression in the reflection. *You okay?* was repeated as Sara spun around in the empty bathroom.

If you were talking right outside, at the stairs, could anybody hear you?

Keesha shrugged. *Under the amplifier? Now? Yes. The music just stopped. A minute ago — No way. It was really loud.* She glanced toward the closed door and grinned. *Don't tell me you lip-read some juicy gossip somebody was whispering! Who's having an affair?*

No affair. Patrick Martinson's going to be murdered when he gives the toast.

Bret found the two of them back at the hors d'oeuvres table. The sun had topped the trees and the riverboat was aglow with paper lanterns. Sara gave him one painful stare as Keesha continued with her hands. *You aren't kidding, are you?*

Just like they got my father. Sara agonized. *You two need to stay safe, out of this mess. It's going to get worse.*

What's going on? Bret signed.

There wasn't time to lie. *I don't know yet, but Dad knew about the bridge collapse being caused by negligence. He was killed after a meeting with T. C-O-V-I-N-G-T-O-N. Dad's gone. They tried to scare Steve off, but the case still continues. Steve told me that Liz's father helped with the investigation.*

Keesha raised her hands. *Those guys . . . nobody would be that stupid, Sara! Not to murder in plain sight . . . on a boat in the middle of the river!*

That's the point. They want it public. Sara

pressed her hands over her mouth to keep down the terror. *The bridge collapse was an accident, but it was because shoddy supplies were used on purpose. Liz's father turned the guy in.* She looked into Bret's worried face. *There are at least two men on this boat with guns under their jackets. One just nodded to that man on the stairs. For some reason, he's part of this. I don't know how.*

A nod doesn't have to mean anything, Keesha replied.

Or it could mean everything! Somebody's going to murder P-A-T-R-I-C-K M-A-R-T-I-N-S-O-N while he makes a toast. If my ears worked and I heard it instead of lip-read it, you'd believe me! Sara stopped as Liz approached with her date.

"I'm supposed to tell you dinner will be served in about half an hour. In about twenty minutes the caterers are going to pass champagne around first so my dad can make a toast. We'll probably get ginger ale, but still — "

Sara touched her arm. "The man who just went back down to the adults? Gray hair. You shook his hand and he patted you on the shoulder. Was his picture in the paper this morning?"

Bret repeated Sara's question.

Liz shrugged. "Maybe. Dad's going to toast him first. That's Mr. Covington. He just retired and the governor gave him some plaque or something."

"Do you know him?"

"Thomas Covington? He's an engineer. He inspects bridges all over the state for the Department of Public Works."

"Shadow Point Bridge?"

"Yeah. Lousy job that time. He feels terrible that he never caught what that creep Gillespie was doing . . . to the bridge or my father. Dad was in Covington's office half the morning listening to his apologies," Liz said.

Where?

"Office? I don't know exactly, but I needed the car and I dropped Dad off in front of the courthouse downtown."

In the same spot where I guessed George Resnik got a traffic ticket for double-parking to run up with the photographs of me, Sara added mentally as fear crept up her spine. In her head her father's hands flew: *Why don't the two of you take in the arts festival at city square? I was at the courthouse this afternoon and the festival's set up across the street in the park. Opening night fireworks over the river.*

Sara squeezed her eyes shut. Her father had been in Thomas Covington's office on Black Saturday. The bridge inspector. The one who said nothing was wrong with Howard Gillespie's work. It was so obvious. Paul Howell had suspected Covington of being part of the cover-up, maybe even confronted him with the information. Three hours later the detective was dead. A month later Patrick Martinson helps implicate Howard Gillespie. The trail again leads to Covington. The last piece of the puzzle. She tried not to panic.

Liz waved to her mother. "Sorry. I've got to go shake more hands, I guess. See you guys later."

Sara looked desperately at Keesha and Bret. *We could do something stupid like spill a drink on the hit men and distract them.*

They're cold-blooded killers, Sara!

Anything massive would cause panic on

the boat. *There must be two hundred people on this thing*, Bret added.

Sara searched the ceiling frantically as if answers were above her. *The wheelhouse.* She tapped her head and turned to her friends. *Pay attention. You both come with me. I'll show you where the killers and the bridge inspector are. Then Keesha, you go to the wheelhouse and tell the captain what's going on. Make it convincing. Tell him you can identify them.*

Bret, watch over things out here while I go into the galley. I'll knock over a tray of champagne or something to get the kitchen into chaos. That'll delay things enough to give the captain time to get the river patrol.

As Keesha nodded Sara began to shake. The Hansel and Gretel crumbs had turned into a trail that might as well have neon signs lighting the way to Thomas Covington. The clues fell horribly into place. *If the inspector's capable of murder here, I'll bet he had one of those two hit men follow my father to the bridge. Dad was set up because he knew too much.*

Bret took her hands between his, then put

his arm around her shoulder. He nodded toward the party. "No time, Sara. Let's take a walk, you guys. We have work to do."

Sara found Thomas Covington without any problem. He was eating shrimp and deep in conversation with a city councilman under a string of Japanese lanterns near the stern. When she was sure Keesha and Bret had taken a close look and could identify him, she moved through the crowd in search of Joe and Mac.

Joe was at the bar drumming his fingers. He didn't make conversation or order a drink. He checked his watch.

He's counting the minutes, Bret signed.

So am I, she replied.

Mac brushed Bret as he passed them on his way to the bow. Keesha nodded that she had seen each one and turned to thread her way through the party and up to the captain.

As she left, the lantern light played over Mac's shoulder. He continued toward Covington. The bridge inspector frowned and turned away from the councilman.

"Get away from me, you damned fool," he said with the clarity of a speech teacher.

Sara glanced at the dance band in full swing. Maybe no one had heard. Maybe Covington never counted on anyone reading lips. It was over in a flash. The hit man continued past Covington and calmly took an hors d'oeuvre from a tray.

It was all so painfully normal. Sara turned to look at Bret, but he'd stepped aside. Instead her steady, clear-eyed gaze accidentally met Thomas Covington's piercing stare head-on. His gray hair gleamed under the lantern light. His eyes were dark, dead as he looked back at her.

Her heart slammed against her ribs. Without thinking, she grabbed Bret's hand. Covington's glance fell to her grasping fingers. The muscles clenched along his jaw and then he turned and moved into the crowd of adults.

He recognized me.

Bret shrugged. *Even if he's been watching you all night, he has no way of knowing whether you know who he is or not.*

But my father . . . Even that wasn't enough. Now he's sending those creeps after poor Mr. Martinson who was only clearing his own good name.

Bret kissed her hard and pulled her into a hug. She wished it would last forever, but just as quickly, he let her go. *Go into the galley and raise hell. Then stay there. Understand? I'll watch the door. Stay under the brightest lights, close to people. Act totally stupid if you have to. Do not leave the galley.*

But you —

I'm nobody, don't worry.

She smiled. *You're somebody. Don't you ever forget it.*

With one last glance, she left Bret to the crowds on the upper deck. He immediately began to talk with kids from the class as if there weren't a thing on his mind but a good time. As she headed for the safety of the galley, she felt his strong steady gaze in the middle of her back, comforting as coals on a hearth.

The galley was in the center of the riverboat. During normal cruises a bank of chest-high doors were propped open so that food could be sold directly from the stainless steel counters inside. For catered affairs, of course, the doors were shut and service was provided to guests at formal tables.

NO ADMITTANCE. EMPLOYEES ONLY. Sara ignored the sign and pushed open the swinging door. She squinted briefly at the harsh overhead light. Hired caterers ringed the stainless counters putting last-minute touches on mounded gourmet side dishes and platters of sliced meats. To her left, trays were laid out, each one lined with champagne glasses. Three waiters had open bottles and were systematically filling the stemware. Others in uniform waited to hoist the trays to their shoulders.

Sara absorbed it all in a heartbeat as she chose the most chaotic place to trip and send glasses spilling, domino-style, off the counter. After a deep breath, she pretended to stumble and plunged forward. As she aimed for the trays, however, a firm grasp caught her around the ribs. She must have screamed. A broad, flat hand slapped over her mouth as she dug her hands into the ironclad forearm lifting her off her feet, pulling her backwards through a swinging door into a pantry.

She threw her head back until skull hit bone and hoped it was the nose of her attacker. As she was unceremoniously dropped, she managed to pivot. From the vinyl floor tiles she looked up into the face of Detective Stephen Howell. Her brother was clean-shaven, combed, and dressed in the same formal tuxedo as the rest of the guests. He crouched and yanked her up with one hand. The other was pressed against his swollen lip.

Chapter 23

Steve let go and put both hands on either side of her face. "It's me! Maybe minus a tooth. You okay?" As she nodded he put his finger to his lips and cocked his head toward the closed pantry door. *Don't fight me. Don't move. Big danger. C-O-V-I-N —*

I know everything. Murder. Soon, Sara replied.

Steve grimaced. *Say again.*

Murder. She lifted her hand as if to sip champagne. *At the toast. Don't serve the drinks! Understand?* She was desperate for Bret. She couldn't risk speech and this was no time for Steve to stumble through her ASL. Her brother furrowed his brows and looked at his watch as Sara swatted at it. *No time to explain, but I know it all. Under-stand?*

Yes!

Two men with guns. They are with C-O-V-I-N-G —

Steve knocked her hands and fumbled. *Bridge . . . inspector?*

Yes. Bridge inspector. He has men who will shoot Liz's dad at the toast. In front of everyone on purpose. I know.

Steve made Sara's sign for *Keesha.*

She pointed to the ceiling. *Wheelhouse. Calling river patrol.*

He looked over their heads. *I sent a cop up there, too.* "The newspaper shot you showed me was the last clue. Dad was tracing *why* the bridge failed. Trying to figure out *how* — it was never caught by inspections, even after collapse. *Understand?*"

She nodded.

"It was the repair crew who found faults, not Covington. *Tonight I realized the inspector must have been paid off by G-I-L-L-E-S-P-I-E.* Paid to approve the bridge. He played odds that the bridge would hold. Nobody to know. Covington inspected the bridge the first time. Arranged to have himself assigned for inspection after the collapse. Of course he said the collapse was accidental. It would have stayed that way . . ."

Except for Dad. Met with him Black Saturday. Courthouse.

Steve nodded. *The minute you left tonight I called here to see* — "if Covington was on the guest list. Got an arrest warrant. Grabbed my tuxedo." *I'm a guest, just like you.* "I can't believe he'd put a hit out here . . ."

If Liz's phone is tapped, he'll know you're not a guest.

Good. If he knows, he'll call off murder. Too — She watched Steve struggle with words.

Risky. Dangerous, she signed for him.

Yes. Steve hugged her. "Martinson delayed the *Buckeye Queen*'s departure till I got out here." Steve glanced at his watch again. "Can you identify Covington's men?"

She nodded. "Bret can, too. He's out there watching them. You stay in here. Promise." *If the inspector sees you —*

He cupped his hand and pushed it forward. *Cop. Me. If the inspector sees me, he'll stop the murder plans.* "No bloodshed." Steve grinned. "Do you feel like kissing Bret?"

Kiss? Sure.

Good. Two times. Once at each gunman, to identify them for me. Don't look for me. When she nodded, he swore, then adjusted his jacket. He pushed the pantry door open.

As she left the galley, she took one quick look at the staff. Lt. Marino was putting chopped parsley on a pasta salad. Sara had no way of knowing if any of the others were undercover police.

The party was still in full swing as Sara walked back among her classmates. As unobtrusively as possible she glanced across the deck until she found Bret. He was standing on the closest staircase with a cigarette between his lips.

You smoke?

Needed an excuse to stand out here. Concern clouded his features. *Get back in the galley,* he signed angrily.

S-T-E-V-E H-E-R-E, she finger spelled against his palm.

Bret coughed. *Brother? On the boat?*

She nodded and took his arm, once again walking among the adult guests, first inside near the buffet tables. As they approached Joe, still at the bar, her heart hammered, but she did as Steve had asked. She ordered a ginger ale. The minute there was no one else close enough to confuse her brother, she looked at Bret and stood on tiptoes. Without telling him first, she put her arm around his neck.

When she came down off her toes, and a breathless kiss, Covington's accomplice had been identified. He gave the teenage lovers a disgusted look. Sara's heart raced and she wished it were from the kiss instead of fear. She didn't dare scan the crowd for Steve.

Her next move was a stroll on the rear deck until she was next to the second gunman. Mac was near the dance band, tapping his foot to what she supposed was a familiar tune. His glance was set squarely on Patrick Martinson as the host chatted with the mayor. Sara snuggled into Bret's arm, then went back up on her toes. This time Bret kissed her first. Her hands shook as Rosemary Marino approached and offered the gunman shrimp from her platter.

The servers arrived with champagne and ginger ale. The soft light played in the tiny bubbles of each fluted glass, hundreds of them, being carried on trays above the heads of the guests. Steve Howell was on the staircase. He looked handsome and happy like dozens of others. Sara hated the fact that he was doing nothing to disguise himself in hopes that the shock of seeing him as a guest would squelch Covington's plans for murder.

Patrick Martinson took the first glass, then skewered the last shrimp from Rosemary Marino's hors d'oeuvres platter. On cue she slipped, sending red cocktail sauce down his shirt front. Sara's last glimpse of Liz's parents were as Mrs. Martinson announced that they'd be right back and led her husband through the crowd in the direction of the stairs. Lt. Marino traipsed behind, bent in apology. Tension kept Sara from smiling.

On the deck above them Sara spotted Steve's rookie partner Hank Allen. He had asked Karen Martinson to dance. The couple moved to Liz. He got both daughters out of harm's way as the riverboat continued to rumble and glide through the water. Sara tried to relax. Both hit men had been identified. Steve had moved his plan into action. All the Martinsons were accounted for.

She crossed to the stern and the edge of the dance floor. Behind her the paddle wheel continued to churn the black water, flecked by the glistening reflection of the swaying lanterns. Time was finally on her brother's side. She had no idea how Steve intended to move in on the men, but she knew it would be subtle. No bloodshed. No disturbing the party.

By now the Martinson family was temporarily — and safely — ensconced in the wheelhouse; soon to return to their oblivious guests. Hopefully someone had radioed for a patrol boat. She would just as soon have dropped all three suspects into the paddle wheel and let the riverboat finish them off.

She leaned gratefully against Bret to take her mind off her brother. He looked like any other guest. She knew her brother was armed, but there was no sign of a weapon.

Lt. Martino appeared on the stairs with her own raised tray of glasses, followed by two more waiters. Neither the bald man nor his stocky associate appeared aware of anything but the party. Neither did her brother. Their icy professionalism kept her breath shallow.

Sara glanced at Thomas Covington. Would he give a signal? His back was to the group. He was talking to a guest, glass in hand. Raise it? Lower it? Drop it to the deck the minute Patrick Martinson returned and proposed his toast? She rubbed her hands over her linen pants. For all she knew he'd recognized Steve, changed his mind, and signaled his goons to cancel.

Sara watched her brother nonchalantly put his hands in his dress pants pockets. Suddenly he frowned. A shadow of doubt crossed his face as he looked at her. Mac, the stocky thug, had moved next to her. Terror stole Sara's breath as Mac signaled the tall, bald, steely-eyed sharpshooter, who slowly moved his hand over his cummerbund. His fingers snaked inside his dinner jacket, but his eyes never left the rookie detective who'd cracked the case. He stared as if he had Steve locked in the crosshairs of a rifle scope.

As public as possible. Take him out as soon as the glasses are raised in that ridiculous toast.

Sara spun to Thomas Covington. He was deep in conversation, his back to the party, but even as he spoke, he raised his glass with infinite precision. She'd been horribly wrong, totally oblivious. She turned back desperately. They weren't after Patrick Martinson. Covington was signaling with his raised glass. The plan was to murder her brother.

Chapter 24

It's Steve. Murder Steve.

Bret's mouth opened before she finished signing. He must have yelled across the stern. Steve turned to him. No screams reached her brain; no gunshots or shattered glass. Instead chaos blurred her vision and filled her head with images of expensive fabric and vibrant colors. The stern of the *Buckeye Queen* emptied as if "Abandon ship!" had been announced. Fluted glasses rolled on their sides or lay in shards under the swaying lanterns while the guests swarmed to the safety of the interior dining room. The paddle wheel stopped turning.

Steve dropped to a stance she'd seen in a hundred action movies. At the same instant

Bret tackled the gunman at the knees. His weapon skittered across the deck and he spun to the port rail. With a single blow Joe shook Bret off as if he were a stray dog. He leapt to the rail, raised his arms, and dove into the inky depths of the Buckeye River. Shelter Island. Mac had said a boat would come later.

Bret dropped and lay motionless at the edge of the dance floor, but Sara knew better than to move a muscle. Her brother stood poised, his own gun aimed directly at Thomas Covington, who had made a great show of protecting the guest he'd been with from the chaos. Steve spoke, then motioned with his weapon.

Covington snickered. Sara caught ". . . ridiculous . . . guest of Patrick and Gloria's . . . not armed."

Steve replied and the bridge inspector took off his jacket as proof. He continued to protest, but stepped forward. Steve shook his head and warned him to stay back.

Sara measured eternity by the rhythmic pounding in her chest. Seconds passed. Minutes? Hours? Covington finally raised his arms in supplication with an apologetic glance at the dance band members, still in their seats. Bret stirred and sat up. She reached for him as a blur in her peripheral vision made her pivot.

For the second time in half an hour, she was yanked off her feet. The stocky accomplice threw his arm around her waist with a force that took her breath. She coughed and struggled while his arm tightened across her diaphragm.

She clawed at the viselike grip. Stars danced. Anguish distorted Steve's features as she tried desperately to stay focused on him. Thomas Covington stepped beside her, cool, dignified. He gave her a single, lingering glance, then spoke to Steve. Her brother shook his head, held his stance and kept his gun aimed. Covington's jaw clenched. He flushed. This time when he spoke he jabbed the air as if he were yelling; the tendons jumped in his neck. The *Buckeye Queen* began to move again.

Light danced on the inky water again as the wheel resumed churning. Pain raced down her ribs. The thug shifted her closer to the rail. He locked his hand over her wrist and nodded at Covington. It became sickeningly clear that she was being bartered as the gunman waited, ready for the signal to drop her into the paddle as it lifted the river through its blades directly below.

Covington leaned over and watched the paddle wheel. Sara craned to watch his mouth but only caught ". . . you wouldn't leave well enough alone, even after Resnik. . . . This time she goes over, Howell." His jaw flexed.

Steve shook his head. He waved his free hand and dropped his weapon. He nudged it forward with his boot. Sara tried to get Bret's attention, but like everyone else, his eyes were locked on Thomas Covington. The bridge inspector walked toward her brother, lunged, picked up the closest gun and aimed point-blank at Steve. In less than a heartbeat Covington nodded.

The thug let go of her. There was a flash. Her nostrils flared at the smell of gunpowder. Unseen, she fell, grabbed for flowers, railing, gripping, slipping as her knuckles burned.

Sara clawed at the air, confused, overboard before anyone had noticed. She landed on her hip, not in the depths of the paddle wheel, but on the roof of the engine housing. The fall broke her momentum and she had enough strength and barely enough time to scramble across the slick surface before she plunged the rest of the way, clear of the wheel, but down into the river.

She surfaced spitting and coughing the Buckeye out of her mouth. It seemed miles above her that Thomas Covington appeared to sail backwards off the stern. He hit the railing with a force that broke the narrow perch where she'd dangled. As he crumbled, her last rational thought was of the stars. She found the one she'd wished on to keep Steve safe.

Chapter 25

Sara spit the river out only to take mouthfuls again. She fought pain, exhaustion, and the current, which had already dragged her from the twinkling lights of the riverboat. She tumbled like laundry in a dryer as she hit the harmless wake of the paddle wheel. Too far from the blades to be threatened, too far to be saved. No one was looking, no one would miss her until . . . Would she show up on the slick, black inky surface?

Her arms ached as she continued to tread water. She was desperate to regain a sense of direction. She fought sobs as she thought about who lay dead or dying on the deck from Covington's last desperate move. Water filled her mouth. She spit, coughed, and sank beneath the surface.

Float! The mental command cleared her head. She bobbed and kicked off her shoes then forced her legs to the surface. She was a rower. Strength, endurance. Coach Barns would be proud. Somebody would throw her a life jacket. Keesha, Liz . . . surely somebody . . . Bret would find her if Steve was . . .

Lead, that was the expression. Arms and legs got so heavy they felt like lead. After all this, she couldn't drown, not in the Buckeye she loved, not because of Covington. He'd gotten Dad, Resnik, maybe Adam Street, maybe Steve. She wouldn't let him win. He couldn't have everybody.

Her hair fanned out along her face and tickled her neck under water like the tendrils of unseen hands. Terror seized her again. The gunman. The swan dive. Joe was out here with her, waiting for a boat off Shelter Island. She began to kick, to force herself to swim. She slapped her left arm, then her right into an exhausted crawl away from the shoreline she knew was the island. Twenty yards from her a campfire glowed. His signal. A boat would come. His boat.

A mile downstream the city lights twinkled but here there was nothing but shadow on shadow and the single glow of banked flames. The boathouses were on the Hillsboro side of the island, the channel side, dark, locked, deserted. She let her legs sink and cried out as her toes sank into silt. The narrow beam of a flashlight skimmed the water. She kicked the river bottom. She wouldn't drown, but she wouldn't let herself be found by the sniper who was out here with her.

She went under again, holding her breath and bobbing beneath the surface, shooting herself up off the silt for a gulp of air. Too much. Too hard. Too tired. After ten minutes her lungs were close to bursting. The agony forced her to the rocks, then to the undergrowth of Shelter Island.

She shoved her hand over her mouth to smother the cough climbing from her throat, and crawled into the pine needles and dirt on the shore. She lay on her back. The flashlight beam danced over the trunks of the pine trees

inches above her head. Sara counted to fifty
and rolled over. Well down the river the
Buckeye Queen still glittered. It hadn't
stopped. Safety first. Back to the marina to
discharge all the passengers. Then they'd
search. Surely they'd come and look for her.
The way the gunman was searching. Bright
beams of light that would find her, warm
her . . .

Sara got to her feet. Stars, a sliver of
moon, city lights. There was enough to see
by. If she kept to the shore, she'd reach the
jogging trail. It ran around the entire perimeter of the island. She'd find the boathouses.
Locked or not, they were familiar territory.
She could break in, set off the alarm, get herself arrested. She laughed through the exhaustion. Any cop would do.

The thought of rescue kept her going as
she stumbled over branches and underbrush,
up the rise from the shore to what she hoped
was the trail. She found it. The pea gravel
hurt the bare soles of her feet but she continued, stumbling along the gentle slope of the
island until the glow of the campfire stopped
her. Close, very close. The same site where

she and Bret had picnicked. She'd kissed him right here, at the campfire, before anyone had been trying to kill her. A real kiss, not one to signal who was a cold-blooded killer.

The signal? The gunman? A figure sat in the fire's glow knees to chest, then jumped to his feet, dusted in shadow. Sara tapped her ears and railed against her deafness, unsure whether she'd made noise. Too easily she could have snapped a twig or set a rock tumbling. She scrambled back down to the waterline. She wrung out her father's soaking jacket, and leaned against the widest tree she could feel.

Find me, she signed to the river with exhausted fingers as tears squeezed between her lashes. *I can't find you.* It was impossible to tell the beam of the river patrol headlamp from something Covington had set up to haul the gunman off Shelter Island. She was drowning in fatigue as she slipped to the ground. She never felt the pine needles rise up under her cheek.

Sara awoke to the wind. The river was churning beyond anything stirred by a paddle wheel. Branches bent as searchlight beams split the night with illumination, brighter than anything from a boat. A police helicopter skimmed the tops of the pines. They were looking for her! She sat up. She was under a dirty wool blanket that scratched her skin. Terror returned and she yanked the blanket off.

The campfire had been fanned into fingers of flame as the whirling blades overhead drove embers into the pine needles. Sara crawled as close as she dared and watched a short, dark-haired figure race in and out of the light as he fought the spread of the fire. Adam Street. Of course. He looked just like his picture as he threw dirt on the flames and raised a fist to the helicopter as needles and undergrowth caught fire on either side of him.

After she began snooping, after Resnik showed up at his camp under the Shadow Point Bridge, Adam Street had moved over here. This campsite was his. No doubt he'd been here somewhere when she arrived with Bret on their picnic.

Sara ran with the blanket. He grabbed it

and smothered the fire, which threatened to fan in all directions. She waved her arms over her head to signal who she was. When she turned back, Adam was back on his haunches, hugging his shoe box to his chest, nervously dragging on a cigarette until its tip glowed. Firelight illuminated them both.

She stood at the edge of the campfire for a moment, then sat across from him. *"I'm deaf,"* Sara said and signed.

He nodded. "I know. You'll have to read my lips. I don't sign like your friends."

So he had seen Keesha and Liz on the trail that first Sunday. He had been up in the bridge girders. He'd watched her sign with Bret right here, no doubt. "My brother Steve has been looking for you." Street stared at her, but there was no indication that he understood her speech.

From the shadows he handed her the linen jacket he had hung on a branch to dry. "My father's," she said.

"Good man." He took a drag from the cigarette. Slowly he nodded. "I've been to your apartment building. Steve wasn't home. Didn't want to scare you."

"You were the one? It's safe now, Adam. The helicopter was looking for me. They'll send a boat. You can go back to Hillsboro House. Back to your safe place," she said with all the clarity she could manage. "Steve can take you back." The hated tears, hot and thick, rolled down her cheeks. "If he's — if he can't, I will. Understand me?"

"Yes." He looked at the trees and stood up, then came back into the light. "It's safe for you, too."

Sara frowned.

"He's gone. He was here while you were asleep, the one who killed your father." He opened the shoe box and handed her what she'd already read. "It wasn't an accident. It was brutal, deliberate. . . . The man who swam here tonight drove the car that afternoon. He killed your father. I saw him get out to make sure he was dead. I was right there. Such a safe place. The trail was closed, bridge over my head. All to myself. Can you understand me?" He touched his mouth.

She nodded. "Boat came for him tonight?"

Adam shook his head. "No boat came. He fell. Tripped on his gun. Shot. Drowned."

The chills returned as she strained to read his lips. She had to grit her teeth to keep them from chattering. "Dead?"

"Now. Yes. Even in the dark I recognized him. I saw him a second time. He hit a man, who was carrying a camera, over the head in the parking lot and dragged him into the bushes."

Sara grimaced. "Resnik. I found his body." Sadly she thought, Now all the pieces fit.

Street pointed to the river and tapped his ear. "Boat's coming. I can hear it."

More light sliced the campsite, this time from the water as searchlights brightened the wedge of river and shore. Sara shielded her eyes and stared into the darkness until Adam tapped her shoulder. "They say to tell you Keesha and Bret are coming. And Steve. They're calling, 'Tell Sara it's Steve.'"

"Steve! Are you sure?"

"Steve Howell. Your brother."

"Steve." She took Adam's hands, then dropped them. "When we go home . . . When you are home, tell Steve everything. It's safe. We're all safe."

The police boat bobbed in the moonlight

as figures scrambled into an inflated raft for the trip through the shallows. The beam followed them. Bret and Steve paddled impatiently for twenty feet. Sara waved. They abandoned ship and plowed thigh-deep, then knee-deep through the water. Sara rushed barefoot down the slope and reached them with the Buckeye lapping their shins. She threw one arm around each neck and they lifted her between them for the strongest, happiest hug of her life.

Suddenly, without a trace, Kimberly Roth has vanished!

Sara is terrified for her friend, and begins a frantic search for clues as to Kim's whereabouts. But these clues lead Sara into deadly danger from which there seems to be no escape.

Read Hear No Evil #2: MISSING!

Every day
Sara Howell
faces mystery, danger ...
and silence.

Sara may be deaf, but she's the only one who hears a friend's cry for help.

When Sara's glamorous friend, Kimberly, is suddenly missing, everyone—even the police department— thinks the "kidnapping" is just a ploy for attention. Only Sara is convinced it's no hoax. But by the time Sara can prove it to the others, the abductors have their eyes on her.

HEAR NO EVIL #2
Missing!
Kate Chester

Coming soon to a bookstore near you.

THRILLERS

Nobody Scares 'Em Like

R.L. Stine

THRILLERS

D.E. Athkins

☐ MC45246-0 Mirror, Mirror $3.50

A. Bates

☐ MC45829-9 The Dead Game $3.99
☐ MC43291-5 Final Exam $3.50
☐ MC44582-0 Mother's Helper $3.99
☐ MC44238-4 Party Line $3.99

Caroline B. Cooney

☐ MC44316-X The Cheerleader $3.50
☐ MC43806-9 The Fog $3.50
☐ MC45681-4 Freeze Tag $3.99
☐ MC45402-1 The Perfume $3.50
☐ MC44884-6 The Return of
　　　　　　　　the Vampire $3.50
☐ MC41640-5 The Snow $2.75
☐ MC45680-6 The Stranger $3.50
☐ MC45682-2 The Vampire's
　　　　　　　　Promise $3.50

Richie Tankersley Cusick

☐ MC43115-3 April Fools $3.50

☐ MC43203-6 The Lifeguard $3.50
☐ MC43114-5 Teacher's Pet $3.50
☐ MC44235-X Trick or Treat $3.50

Carol Ellis

☐ MC44768-8 My Secret Admirer $3.50
☐ MC44916-8 The Window $3.50

Lael Littke

☐ MC44237-6 Prom Dress $3.50

Christopher Pike

☐ MC43014-9 Slumber Party $3.50
☐ MC44256-2 Weekend $3.99

Edited by T. Pines

☐ MC45256-8 Thirteen $3.99

Sinclair Smith

☐ MC46126-5 Dream Date $3.99
☐ MC45063-8 The Waitress $3.99

Available wherever you buy books, or use this order form.

Scholastic Inc., P.O. Box 7502, 2931 East McCarty Street, Jefferson City, MO 65102

Please send me the books I have checked above. I am enclosing $ _____ (please add
$2.00 to cover shipping and handling). Send check or money order — no cash or C.O.D.s please.

Name _____ Age _____

Address _____

City _____ State/Zip _____

Please allow four to six weeks for delivery. Offer good in the U.S. only. Sorry, mail orders are not
available to residents of Canada. Prices subject to change.　　　　　　　　　　T1095